A ROSE BLOOMS AMONG THE THORNS

Cissy Hunt

PublishAmerica
Baltimore

ISBN: 978-1-61582-045-0 (softcover)
ISBN: 978-1-4489-9232-4 (hardcover)
PUBLISHED BY PUBLISHAMERICA, LLLP
www.publishamerica.com
Baltimore

Printed in the United States of America

DEDICATION

This book is dedicated to all women who have ever experienced domestic violence of any type; be it physical, sexual, mental, or emotional abuse. I pray it points you toward hope, healing and a new life.

ACKNOWLEDGMENT

I would like to thank my husband, Ray, who has stood beside me and walked with me through every dark path and obstacle that has come my way. You are my "White Night," my defender, my encourager. Thank you for believing me when I didn't believe in myself.

I would like to thank my dear friend Debora who with out her help, prayers, encouragement, and many late hours reading, subjections, and help editing this book would probably still be a dream. Thank you my dear friend for more than I could ever put into words on this piece of paper.

I would like to thank my mother who taught me strength during adversities. I've seen you go through some things that could have destroyed a weaker woman, yet, you always stood strong, like your mother before you. Thank you for your love, support, and lessons on life.

A ROSE AMONG THE THORNS

Alone in the darkness, she cannot see
She hears danger, moving all around
With shouts and intimidations it calls her name.
Each curse and threat cuts deep
Like the thorns on a bush
Ripping and tearing self-worth to shreds

Running—Running—Running
She's afraid, of what it'll do
Eyes swollen and face black and blue
She runs under the cover of darkness.
Carrying with her the latest angry marks!
Running—stumbling—falling

She listens, in the night
As it slowly moves in on her
Laughing—taunting—threatening
Oh, how those thorns can hurt!
Ripping—cutting—tearing
Self-respect damaged and torn

Warm hands reach passed the thorns
Deep within to the tiny withering bud
Embraced by Great Healing hands
The tiny bud begins to heal and
A beautiful rose blooms among the thorns
In the nailed scared healing hands

CHAPTER 1

LaRae's hands trembled as she slowly hung up the phone. She rose from her chair—the caller's mysterious words still fresh in her thoughts. Gazing out her apartment window she pondered over the conversation. The familiar scenery spread out before her as the autumn colored leaves danced about in the breeze. LaRae watched as a slender woman who appeared to be in her middle twenties carefully took the hand of the young girl standing beside her. Before crossing the street below, she waited for traffic to clear and then headed for the same apartment building LaRae has lived in for the past year and three months. She recognized them as the mother and daughter who occupied the apartment below her. Though she kept her own identity concealed from others, not allowing anyone too close, she made it a point to know as much as she could about the people living around her.

Watching the mother and young child brought back memories—memories of when she first left James. Memories that left her frightened and unmistakably void of all emotions except fear. He had treated her like a small child, making her believe she didn't even know how to cross the street by herself without written directions. In time James had totally dominated her life to the point of telling her what to do, when to do, what to wear and whom she could speak with. She was allowed no friends and no contact with anyone outside of James.

In the beginning of the marriage he would give little excuses for why she could not visit with her family or friends. At first, her visits would always coincide with important business functions or he would claim he forgot and made dinner reservations, therefore canceling out any plans she may have had. He started demanding she be home when he called or wanted her home when he was home. Each day he took away a little bit more of her freedom until one morning she woke up to find she had no freedom; she was a prisoner in her own home. That's when she knew she had to escape, no matter the cost she had to get away and find her independence. She had to try and find herself.

The reality of the resent phone conversation brought her back to the present. Gradually, fear begins to creep in like the cold on a winter's night. The color drained from her face and her whole body shivered as the totality of it hit home with her.

"No, no, no not again, please not again," she cried.

Looking about the room, the urge to run completely consumed her. She had stayed at her present residence too long. Way too long—months now! Her awareness of her surroundings was growing more intense. The urge to look over her shoulder grew stronger with every passing minute. Had she become careless? She thought she had been so careful this time. She started pacing back and forth across the bedroom.

"Where did I mess up? Did I take the same route home too many times? Did I buy gas or groceries at the same place too many times? Where, oh where did I mess up? How did he find me?" LaRae kept agonizing over her present situation. Even though it wasn't James's voice on the phone, she knew it was someone working on his behalf and he now had her phone number.

Knowing what to do, she walked to the closet, removed her clothes from the hangers, and tossed them on the bed. For over five years now, LaRae had gone through this horrible scenario countless times. First came the phone call, then the hasty packing, and finally driving off to who knows where in the middle of the night, never to look back, again. LaRae began to cry as she slowly sank to the floor.

"How could you be so careless? How could you let your guard

down like that?" She kept chastising herself.

LaRae remained perplexed and unsettled over the phone conversation she had a few minutes ago. After thoroughly reviewing her actions, she knew she had been very careful to cover her tracks with the caution of a hunted animal. The horrors of the past five years had taught her to always be cautious and always be watchful for anything out of place, anything that wasn't quite right. She had purposely taken assignments that would take her far from home and to remote areas, so that no one who had known her back then would even think to look for her in those areas. She was in one of those areas now and, yet, somehow James had gotten through.

There was something not entirely right about the man on the phone and how he pushed for answers to his questions. He said he was updating employee files for Regions Memorial Hospital. He needed information for some forms that seemed to have been overlooked. If the files weren't completed he could not give his approval for her next paycheck. The information he said he needed updated was current address, social security number and a copy of her driver's license. It was at that point in the conversation LaRae realized the man on the other end of the phone line was seeking her identity and hung up the phone. The old fear of being trapped like an animal gripped her.

After the reality of the whole phone conversation sunk in, LaRae begin to tremble. In stark realization, she shrieked. "For my next paycheck! How could I be so foolish? I'm not an employee of Regions Memorial Hospital!" An independent nationwide company that supplied skilled nursing personnel to hospitals that were understaffed employed LaRae. Employment was offered to individuals in areas of specialty nursing, or people like her who had their degree in nursing and computer science.

Slowly LaRae stood to her feet and rummaged through the clothes remaining in the closet. With each look she would inevitably pull out another dress, skirt, blouse or jacket of which she absolutely had to take with her, then in turn go through boxes of shoes and handbags to make each ensemble complete. With an emerald green dinner dress in her hand, she turned to place it on the bed. Noticing the bed was already piled high with a variety of clothes, each in a distinctive color and texture of material, she compared the pile of clothes on the bed to the available space in the two remaining suitcases. She glanced at the two trunks, already packed to capacity, placed beside the closet and made a mental note of what was packed in each.

"I give up!" she exclaimed.

She was frustrated with the whole ordeal of having to pick and choose and then pack up what she could of her personal belongings.

Looking at the remaining clothes in the closet she knew that anything she left behind would be lost to her forever. Knowing she could never return to this area again—because returning to the same area was the careless mistake that allowed him to find her the last time—she made her final decisions. A shiver passed through her body when she remembered how she barely escaped with her life.

She glanced at the clock on the bedside table.

"Oh, no, it's already three o'clock."

LaRae was frantic because she was running out of time. She had wanted to be through with all her packing, and have all her bags and boxes in her small SUV and ready to leave just after dark. Once again she would make her hurried departure under the cover of darkness.

"Stop it right now!" LaRae mentally chastened herself, sternly.

Because fear had once more raised its ugly head and had a vicious grip on her thoughts, she forced her mind to return to the present and concentrate on the task at hand instead of the fear that persistently pulled her to where she did not want to go; back to the past; back to a previous time that was shrouded in horror, pain, and humiliation. With a renewed sense of determination, she once again returned to her packing and sorting. She finally settled on taking all but four of her remaining outfits, but had to leave several pairs of shoes and handbags behind.

*

With an unyielding look of determination, James Ashcroft glared at the occupant in the chair across from him. His jaw hard as granite, he was finding it difficult to control the smoldering anger just under the exterior of his stern expression. However, Gilbert Garth had been in the business too long to allow such intimidations to bother him; he thought how that look would probable buckle most men.

"Well, have you found her yet, Mr. Garth?"

In his long career as a private investigator, Gilbert Garth had heard that short question many times. Clients tend to ask it when an investigation seemed to come to a standstill and their voices became tenser with each repetition. But not this client, his voice had never altered, even though it had been nearly a year and a half since he had last asked the question. A lot of control in this one, Gilbert thought, as well as an unrelenting mysterious determination pushing him onward.

"I have a lead," Gilbert replied, allowing his own suspicions to show in his voice, as he watched James take a drag from the cigarette in his hand. James looked at him with his burning dark eyes. Even though the investigator was no longer unsettled by that look, he could see the smoldering wrath just below the surface in them.

"A lead you don't exactly trust?" James questioned warily.

Garth nodded, not in agreement, but rather in observance of his clients reply; a reply not surprising to him since he had come to know this client.

"It didn't come through any of my regular sources. If you remember, I warned you this could take awhile."

"I remember." was the controlled reply.

"Well, it should have taken a long time. But this morning, out of the blue, I received a newspaper clipping. The kind of thing some small town papers print about local activities."

James waited silently, his broad shoulders slowly tightening under the dark colored jacket; his hard face gave a look of danger that was intensified by his rigid stillness. Gilbert thought briefly of the man he first met years ago, and how little he had changed over the years. He was still a very ominous, demanding man; yet his meticulous appearance presented a man very much in control of himself and his environment. However, Gilbert knew the danger that was held in check just below the surface. It was because of this knowledge and several extreme outbursts in the beginning that he came close to giving notice to this client.

"The newspaper clipping," the investigator went on, "was on the back of an obituary a friend had sent me about another friend of mine of which I had lost contact with years ago. It was a small article about a local hospital opening its new cardiac care unit. They had hired a cardiac care nurse on a temporary basis to set up the clinic as well as the new computer programs for the unit, and train the staff nurses on all the new equipment. The nurse was LaRae Jones."

"Did the article have a photograph?" James asked trying to act nonchalantly.

"Yes, I made you a copy of it."

Gilbert handed his client an envelope containing a copy of the newspaper article with photograph. James Ashcroft placed the envelope on his desk without opening it and continued to question Gilbert Garth.

"Did you check it out?" For the first time there was a hint of strain in James' deep, even voice.

"By phone, yea. She was working there until a week ago. The hospital said she's accepted another assignment, but they weren't willing to give any other information. I need to go out there and pick up her trail." Gilbert did not relay to his client at this time that he had, also, spoken to her over the phone. And it was most likely this conversation that caused her to run again.

"You don't trust the information?"

"What I really don't trust Mr. Ashcroft, is you," Gilbert said to himself suppressing the urge to speak his mind as he so often does.

"That young woman is running from something or someone and is taking great strides to not be found," he continued to think.

"Like I told you before, I think she's running from something or someone, and I can't find out what," Gilbert replied.

James tensed at those words, for he knew what and whom she was running from.

"It appears she uses her own name on the job, but uses cash and a false name for all her traveling and lodgings; that's what makes it so difficult to find her. And that's why it's so important that I go out there before her trail gets cold."

James rose from his desk and stepped to the window, gazing out at the city below. Without turning, he said in a low calloused voice, "You've gotten this close once before, and lost her."

Garth knew what he was being asked. And it wasn't only his professional pride at stake here, but a purely special concern he had developed in this woman. He knew this woman did not want to be found and he wanted to know why.

In a low voice, he answered, "I don't mean to lose her this time, Mr. Ashcroft. I have contacts that will help me; I'll pick up her trail."

Gilbert Garth rose from his chair, "I'll let you know if I find out anything."

He placed his hat on his head, walked out of the office, and closed the door behind him.

*

LaRae slowly walked from her apartment closing the door behind her to the elevator down the hall. She quickened her steps once outside the apartment building and hurriedly crossed the street to her blue SUV, already packed with what would fit of her personal possessions. Opening the door and pulling the driver's seat forward, LaRae placed her overnight case on the back floorboard. She would not give in to the temptation to take one last look back.

LaRae quickly settled into the driver's seat, started the engine, and drove down the long driveway between the apartment buildings to the main road. She did not try to hold back the tears that had gathered in the corners of her blue eyes. Once at the end of the driveway she stops her car and begins to sob bitterly. LaRae sat and cried until she could cry no more. Taking tissues from her purse, she gently wiped the last remaining tears from her face.

"When can I truly have a home? When can I put down roots and never have to look over my shoulder again? You know that can never be until you can conquer the monster of your past that has haunted you for all these years," she scolded herself. Then, she laughed bitterly knowing a scared rabbit only runs and hides. One brief glance at the reflection of her face in the rearview mirror told her story—especially her eyes.

"You have got to stop this. You can't cry all the way to Texas. Now, get it together. You will not shed another tear!" She reprimanded loudly. There was no time to worry about her appearance; she had a long drive laid out before her. She knew it would be dark soon and no one would be able to notice her red puffy eyes, anyway.

LaRae shifted her car into drive. Easing out onto the main road, she proceeded west into town where she would take Main Street eastward to the interstate.

"Okay, it's three point five miles to Main Street."

LaRae knew it was precisely three point five miles from the apartment driveway to the only traffic light on Main Street. She knew this because consistent fearfulness always had her planning an escape route wherever she resided at the time. Therefore, she had measured the distance not long after her arrival.

LaRae reached over, turned the radio on, tuned it in to her favorite "Oldies" station, and turned the volume up loud…loud enough that it would interfere with her thinking. The one thing she did not want to do was to think—especially about James. Thinking about James always pulled her back into the past—the horrible past—and that was the last place she wanted to be—in the past with James.

While sitting at the only traffic light in the small town, LaRae searched through her purse for her address book. Finding the little pink book, she placed it in a holder in the console between the front seats beside her cell phone. She had decided to wait until after traveling a little over halfway through her trip before placing a second call to her dearest and longest friend Cindy.

LaRae talked with Cindy in a brief conversation just a few minutes after completing her packing. After loading the suitcases in her automobile, she informed Cindy of some time off and a sudden decision to come for a short visit. It had to be a short visit because LaRae would never take the chance of Cindy being harmed. LaRae debated over and over about making the trip because of the cost if James ever made the connection between her and Cindy or found her in Texas at Cindy's home.

Her friend, Cindy and their longstanding friendship had meant everything to LaRae and she did not want to place her in a dangerous situation. Yet, putting Cindy in harm's way would be exactly what LaRae would be doing if perchance James ever found out about their friendship. Did she want to do that? So far LaRae has been able to keep their closeness concealed from him.

Maybe she should drive strait on through and not stop, not take the chance of James finding out about Cindy and taking his revenge out on her—like he had on others close to her so many times before. LaRae knows him well and he had always taken away everyone and everything that was important to her. She could not bear it if anything ever happened to Cindy. They had been closer then sisters since childhood. She supposed she could always tell Cindy there had been a change in plans and her new assignment had to start sooner than she thought, but right now she really needed to be with her dear friend.

LaRae now focused her attention on the traffic light that had just turned green. She eased her car through the intersection and drove slowly through town. When she found herself on the outskirts, she increased her speed rapidly.

Driving through the night she let her mind drift to her childhood days, back to the time she had met her best friend. LaRae laughed as she reminisced about the day as if it were just yesterday. How they became best friends from such a rocky beginning was a wonder to her.

LaRae remembered one morning she had climbed up in a persimmon tree that grew beside the roadway and sit in a fork of two branches and leaned against the tree. While sitting there, a girl her own age came along riding a bicycle on the road passing under the long branches of the tree. The girl couldn't see her because the branches were heavy laden with leaves. LaRae started picking the green persimmons off the branches around her and tossing them at the girl on the bicycle. She was tossing the persimmons ever so gently because she wanted the girl to think they were just naturally falling out of the tree on her. Each time the girl would ride under the tree LaRae would toss a couple of persimmons at her. Soon the girl started riding past the tree on the far side of the road, yet still LaRae would toss the green persimmons at her.

Finally the girl had had enough and after throwing down her bike and making a basket with the tail of her shirt, she started gathering the green persimmons from off the roadway. Not knowing exactly where LaRae was hiding in the tree the girl start bombarding the tree with the persimmons and throwing them back in the direction in which they had come from. Soon the girl heard, "Okay, okay, I surrender, I surrender," coming from the tree.

"Come down out of that tree now," the girl demanded with her hands placed firmly on her hips.

"Okay, I'm coming down," LaRae responded back.

LaRae climbed down from the tree rubbing the red whelps on her arms and legs left by the green persimmons the girl sailed back through the branches and introduced herself.

"My name is LaRae Jones. What's yours?"

"My name is Cindy, Cindy Keller. Why were you throwing these green persimmons at me?" she asked holding a persimmon up for LaRae to see.

"I was just trying to get your attention to see if you wanted to play with me."

"Well, why didn't you just ask me?"

"I don't know," LaRae responded. "Can I ride your bike?"

LaRae took an instant liking to Cindy; their spirits connected. After a few more minutes of conversation, Cindy gave up her bike for LaRae to ride and they have been close friends ever since that day.

After driving late into the night, LaRae decided to stop for the night; the day's events had taken their toll on her. She was exhausted physically and emotionally, and could not drive another mile tonight. She decided she would find a motel, get some rest, and start out early the next morning.

Making a decision to stop, she came upon a lonely looking motel set back off the roadside. The quaint plain looking place was the first she had come across in quite awhile. At first she was not going to stop, but then thought better of the idea, once she saw the driveway and parking area curved behind the main buildings.

"This is the only place I've seen for awhile and I'm tired, and don't want to try and drive any further tonight." She stated.

Not too long after making her decision, and maneuvering her SUV down the crude rocky driveway, she was entering her assigned room.

LaRae quickly showered and settled into bed, hoping maybe she would be able to sleep this night. It had been a long time since she had been able to sleep peacefully for more than a couple of hours at a time during the night. She was afraid to sleep. Sleep always brought with it dreams.

She whispered, "No, not dreams, nightmares!"

LaRae had not been asleep more than a couple of hours when she awoke in a panic. She was gasping for air trying hard to catch her breath. Her nightgown was drenched in sweat. Her whole body quaked uncontrollably like a volcano about to erupt.

"Why won't you leave me alone? I just want to have a life." LaRae screamed. She was curled up in a ball rocking back and forth, crying bitterly.

"Why won't you stop?"

She closed her eyes forcefully as she tried to push the memories away. They were a brutal invasion of unavoidable reminders of unhealed wounds James had left her with. She could feel a lump of terror inside of her growing larger as she struggled to overcome it. She could almost hear James' taunting, accusing words that always left her frightened and paralyzed with fear. The cold echoes of those memories made a sudden new fear rise inside of her.

"Go away, go away. I don't want you here. Leave me alone. When will I ever have peace? Why can't you just leave me alone?" LaRae cried.

After taking another shower and changing her nightgown, LaRae tried once more to resume sleep hoping it would be restful but knowing any sleep would not be peaceful, and she was right. On and off throughout the night, her sleep was restless and filled with dreams and nightmares of the past. Past hurts and humiliations danced in and out of her mind as she fought her way back...back to wakefulness.

Finally giving up on sleep, LaRae showered, dressed comfortable for the day's trip, and placed her luggage back into her SUV. Since she would be traveling most of the day, finding a place to eat a nourishing breakfast would be nice.

Placing her overnight bag back in its place behind the front seat she got in her SUV and headed out of the motel parking lot. It wasn't long before she spotted a diner not far from the motel. The sign on the window read, *Breakfast Served Until 10A.M.* She was famished and pulled in the driveway of the diner and parked her vehicle near the back of the restaurant behind a shed that blocked its exposure to the highway. She entered the building and out of habit surveyed the room; as always she searched out an open table in the back corner.

After being seated by a young dark haired girl of LaRae's same height, she ordered blueberry pancakes, sausage, grits, and orange juice. She asked that coffee be brought while she was waiting on her meal. There were not very many people in the little diner, but then again it was near mid-morning and no doubt most that frequented the eatery had already come and gone. Being that this community seemed to be a farming community, most people were up before the crack of dawn and had long since already eaten their breakfast.

LaRae paid her tab, left the restaurant and headed for her vehicle. The sky was cloudy and it was beginning to sprinkle rain. She quickened her steps through the parking lot barely noticing the white sedan parked parallel on a side street not far from her own vehicle. After settling into the seat and buckling the seat belt, she scrutinized the sky and determined by the gathering of the dark clouds she was in for some bad weather.

She backed out of the parking space and headed toward the street that would lead her to the highway out of town. Feeling alert and refreshed after a nourishing breakfast, she was soon traveling down the highway that would take her to her friend's hometown. Adjusting her speed to the required limit, she turned on cruise control and kept a watchful eye on the threatening sky.

LaRae tuned the radio in to a local station in hopes of getting the latest weather information. Finally finding a channel that was giving warnings of severe weather coming her way, she looked at her watch and could tell she was still a good two hours away from Cindy's house. Maybe she could make it to the town before the one Cindy lived in before the storm hit, she thought. She pressed on the accelerator and speeding up begins to pass the cars in front of her. She was not going much over the speed limit and hoped she would not be stopped.

Continuing on her journey, ever watchful for the blue lights that could start flashing in her rearview mirror at any time she noticed a white car traveling closely behind her. Every time she would pass the vehicle in front of her, the white car behind her would too. Every time she changed lanes, the white car would also—making sure to always keep one car in between her and it.

Panic begins to creep in. LaRae didn't think it was by coincidence that the white vehicle was behind her and behaving as it was. She decided to try and see if she could tell who was driving the white car. She waited till she came upon a couple of cars traveling fairly close to one another. She moved out around the first one and sure enough the white car moved out behind her. When she got a little pass the first vehicle she quickly swung her vehicle in front of that car squeezing in between it and the one in front almost causing the car behind her to hit her in the backend. There was not enough room for the white car following her to do the same thing. Whoever was driving the white car had to pass. She looked over to see if she could recognize the driver, but by this time it was raining fairly hard and all she could see was a man's silhouette. She didn't know who the man could be, but she was certain of one thing. It was not James. She would know his image anywhere.

Although frightened, she knew she had to keep her senses about her. It was beginning to storm. The wind had picked up and gust shook her vehicle from time to time. She didn't know what to do. She looked at her watch again and saw she was still too far from the nearest town to obtain any help from the local authorities. Whoever the person was following her, she was sure it had something to do with James. She could not lead him near Cindy. Watching for any and all exits off the interstate she finally saw one up ahead of her. The white car had slowed down and was waiting for her to move back in front of it. LaRae kept her distance and kept slowing her own speed till she got near the exit. As soon as the white vehicle passed the exit, LaRae made a sharp swerve and exited the interstate. When she did so, the white car put on the brakes and moved onto the shoulder of the road. LaRae kept going and turned down the first dirt road she came upon and quickly backed in and parked her car behind some tall bushes.

Trembling, she turned the ignition off and sat in stone silence while watching for any sign of the white car. After collecting her thoughts, she remembered the white car was the same one she had briefly noticed at the diner parked on a side street not far from where she had been parked. The realization of knowing someone was indeed following her, made her even more conscious that James had not given up.

LaRae didn't see any sign of the white car while parked on the dirt road waiting out the storm. After a couple of hours, she decided to continue on her trip. The wind had calmed down and so had she. The rain had subsided and the storm clouds were dissipating. She proceeded cautiously out from behind the bushes and made her way back to the interstate to continue her journey.

CHAPTER 2

The remainder of her trip went smoothly and uneventful with no signs of the white sedan. Stopping only for gas and a quick snack, she arrived in the town of Crosstimber late that night. While sitting at a traffic light on the outskirts of town, LaRae looked at her watch to check the time.

"It's nine o'clock. It's kind of late. Wait! Cindy may still be at her friend's shop. She had written to me not long ago about helping her friend remodel an old store he had bought with the intentions of opening an antique boutique," she suddenly remembered.

She quickly rummages through her purse for the last letter she had received from Cindy. Finding the letter, LaRae quickly scanned over it.

"Yes here we go; the shop is located on the corner of King Street and Maple. 402 King Street is the exact address." After placing the letter on the dashboard of her SUV, she repeated the address once more out loud to memorize it.

"402 King Street, on the corner of King and Maple."

The traffic light turned green and as she eased her SUV through the intersection, LaRae quickly looked for a street name.

"Apple and King. Great, I'm on King Street at least."

LaRae drove slowly down King Street, checking the street signs as she drove through each intersection. While once again waiting for a traffic light to turn green, LaRae considered the sequence of streets she had already passed,

"Pine, Oak, Elm, and this one is Beech. I've got to be getting close to Maple. There's not that many tree names left."

Once again the light turned green and LaRae continued to drive to the next intersection. Slowing for the traffic light, she read the street sign,

"Maple!" She exclaimed! "Well, it's about time."

LaRae quickly scanned the name and building numbers of each shop. She noted that the only antique shop was through the intersection and on the right corner of the street.

"This has to be it. I don't see another antique shop on this block," she thought as she looked for a parking space.

Finding an empty space right in front of the antique shop, LaRae eased her SUV into it. She quickly removed the barrette that had been holding her long blonde hair up off her neck and let it fall to its length below her shoulders. She pulled a brush through it several times before checking her makeup in the rearview mirror. She was now ready to meet her longtime friend, Cindy.

Entering the shop and stopping a few feet inside the door to search the dimly lit interior for the familiar face of her friend, she noticed a woman dressed in jeans and a blue T-shirt across the room, with her back toward the door, having a discussion with a man. She judged the man to be a carpenter from his kaki colored clothing and the tool belt about his waist. Even though LaRae had not seen Cindy for about six years, she would know her friend anywhere and the woman in deep conversation with the man was definitely Cindy. While LaRae patiently waited for the man and woman to finish their conversation, she took the opportunity to closely examine the shop and the work that had been completed and came to the conclusion that this will be a very charming little shop when it is completed.

Cindy was slender in build. She looked to be about six to seven inches taller than LaRae, which would put her height about five feet six or seven inches.

"She is still much taller than me. Somewhere through these years

I quit growing and she didn't," LaRae thought to herself, comparing in a nearby mirror, her own height of only five feet. Cindy's shoulder length, light auburn hair was pulled back loosely in a ponytail.

"I'd know that head of hair anywhere," she said softly to herself laughing at a humorous memory of long ago. Cindy used to hate the red shade of her hair. It was too red to be considered blond but too light to be considered auburn. So, one summer day they had created the shade of sunburned blond. LaRae giggled softly at the memory.

"Rae, Rae, earth to LaRae."

Surprised, LaRae jumped from the sound of the familiar voice.

"Where were you?" Cindy asked as she gave LaRae a hearty welcome hug.

"Oh, I was with a girl with sunburned blond hair," LaRae laughingly responded as she returned the hug.

"If I remember correctly at the time I was with a sunburned girl with blond hair," Cindy lightheartedly replied.

The two friends laughed excitedly as they continued over and over to embrace one another. LaRae noticed the tears of joy that had gathered in the corners of Cindy's green eyes—making them shine like deep green emeralds, LaRae thought as she continued to watch them sparkle and dance in the light of the room.

"It has been way to long since we've been together," Cindy exclaimed while pulling LaRae to a nearby sofa.

"I know, and I know that telephone calls and letters are just not the same as being together, but time seems to just get away from me," LaRae replied a little defensively, remembering the main reason she had put distance between Cindy and herself.

"James," LaRae shuttered at the thought of the man.

"Cindy! Do you want us to go ahead and start on the upstairs when we finish here?" The man Cindy was talking to earlier interrupted the women's conversation.

As the man walked toward them, Cindy noticed LaRae trying to hide a yawn and remembered her friend's long journey and responded. "No, Harry, y'all go ahead and finish up down here and then call it a day."

LaRae watched as Cindy handed the man she called Harry a set of keys, while giving him detailed instruction for tomorrow morning's work.

"Come on let's get out of here so you can relax." Cindy said as she gently pulled LaRae out the door.

"Do you remember the way to the ranch?" Cindy asked, as she looked both ways before crossing the street to her black four-wheel drive truck.

"I know it's been a while since you've been out to the ranch, so just follow me, I'm in the black truck parked right across the street."

LaRae maneuvered her SUV in behind Cindy's black truck and followed it to the outskirts of town. She turned right onto the highway and drove for another ten miles. Then, slowing down, her left turn signal started blinking on and off. After turning off the highway and traveling a short distance, the paved road turned to gravel. LaRae slowly maneuvered her own vehicle down the bumpy dusty road for about another two miles following closely behind Cindy. Cindy's truck made a right turn in front of her and traveled a short distance before coming to a stop in the driveway of the ranch house, LaRae remembered visiting not long after Cindy's marriage to Nick. LaRae pulled her vehicle into a parking space beside Cindy's black truck and turned off the ignition.

The heavy wooden door that opened into the foyer was the same as it had been all those many years ago when she and Cindy had swung it wide while chasing Nick with water balloons.

"You can shower and change your clothes in here." Cindy pointed LaRae to the guest bedroom with an attached bath.

"While you're freshening up I'll fix us something to eat."

With those words, Cindy headed toward the kitchen and LaRae followed Cindy's directions and entered the guest bedroom, placing her luggage on a cedar chest located at the foot of the bed.

A short while later LaRae entered the living room wearing a blue Muslin nightgown with a matching robe fastened loosely about her waist with a cloth belt. She pulled her still damp hair back with a barrette. Cindy had positioned two low tables in front of the fireplace with large pillows in front of them; she sat down at the closest one to her. On each table, Cindy had placed a salad, a bowl of soup, a sandwich, and a glass of milk.

"I know you would prefer something light after traveling all day," Cindy expressed as she entered the room with silverware in hand.

"Yes, you're right," LaRae smiled. "You remember my preferences well."

During the meal the two friends spoke quietly of days gone by reminiscing of the day they first met and the many years of friendship that followed. Then each of them took turns catching the other up on the different events of their lives since their last visit. LaRae was careful to avoid the subject of James and the occurrences of the last few years; she was just too tired to deal with such an emotional conversation at this time.

Knowing LaRae was purposely avoiding the incident that had caused her to come running to her best friend, Cindy kept the conversation light. She hoped there would be plenty of time later for that discussion. Cindy was almost certain, even though LaRae had never mentioned anything of James and their divorce; he was the reason she was here and the reason for the haunted look, so evident, in her dear friend's eyes.

When the ladies finished eating, Cindy cleared away their dishes. "Need help?" LaRae asked trying to cover a yawn.

"No, you look as if you could fall asleep standing up. You just relax," she said smilingly, trying to mask her concern for her friend.

From the kitchen out of view of LaRae, Cindy took the time to observe her friend closely; she could see LaRae was exhausted, she had deep, dark circles under her eyes and her face had a pale washed out look about it. Yet, there was something else, something not quite right. Fear was hidden behind those once bright joyful eyes.

After saying good night, LaRae took the stairs up to her room and upon entering she softly closed the door behind her. She was tired, very tired! Yet, she was afraid; terrified to sleep for when she was asleep she was not aware; aware of her surroundings. Since leaving James, she has had to be very cautious and always conscious of everything around her. Every strange sound, every odd movement would set her instantly into alert mode. Here, everything was strange, every noise, every movement, was new to her—therefore, she could not let her guard down, she had to constantly be watching and listening.

Noticing the French doors across the room with a balcony beyond, LaRae stepped through the doors onto the balcony careful to stay in the shadows. Swirls of fog obscured her view of the scenery below. Delicate lifeless fingers moved stealthily among the plants in the garden giving the landscape a disturbing appearance. She shivered even though the night air was warm and peppered with the scent of the mixture of flowers, causing her to pull her robe tightly about her. She imagined the history this place could tell if it could talk. It had been Nick's great grandfather's home.

The moment she thought about history her mind turned toward James. She didn't want him to intrude on her time here with Cindy, but as always she felt vulnerable, fragile, like a young child. She had tried for many years to toughen herself against his accusations and threats, but so far it had been to no avail.

A memory, clear as if it had happened yesterday, imposed itself on her and stole away what composure she had left. She had been newly married and learning how to be a wife. Over and over James had yelled and cursed at her slow accomplishments of doing things the way he liked them done. After one particular evening, she was late getting home from a meeting. As a result, the evening meal was late. She sat at the kitchen table with tears streaming down her cheeks after many attempts of hurriedly trying to fix a suitable meal. She rubbed her eyes and looked at James, as he entered the room, for support and love. All she could remember was the anger on his face; his feet braced apart, his hands clenched at his hips. He ordered her into the kitchen, and with threats and profanity he grabbed her by her arm and hurled her through the kitchen door with no more concern than he would have for a rag doll.

A sound penetrated LaRae's mind, pulling her away from her memories. She blinked, focusing on her surroundings, trying to slow the rapid beating of her heart.

"Rae?"

She turned from the railing and saw Cindy walking toward her. She squeezed her eyes shut, taking a minute before acknowledging her presence until she had control of her emotions.

"I thought you were indeed fast asleep." Cindy commented after finding her out on the balcony.

LaRae out of instinct automatically stepped back a few paces. Her heartbeat had not slowed its frantic pace, and she had to force herself to take deep slow breaths of the country air that smelled of heavenly dew and wildflowers.

"And I thought you were long fast asleep." LaRae replied softly.

"I guess neither of us could sleep." Cindy softly laughed

"Sleeping in a strange bed does that to me." And the fact I can't allow myself to relax, she thought, but kept it to herself.

*

Two days later Gilbert Garth called with satisfaction in his voice still mixed with a thread of doubt.

"I think I might have a solid lead," he reported. "Her neighbor, in the apartment building—a single mother with a young child that was very talkative—related she'd moved to somewhere in the Ozark Mountains."

"Find her," James ordered, holding his voice steady with an effort.

"I'll leave out tomorrow morning for the Midwest, the Ozarks"

"Don't approach her at all; just find out where she is. Then call me."

There was a short pause on the line then Gilbert heard his employer speak.

"You've got that?" James growled.

Gilbert hung up the phone without giving the last comment an answer, and walked slowly back to his car.

James sat down behind the desk, his gaze fixed on the folded copy of the newspaper clipping lying on the blotter. He watched his hands reach out and very slowly unfold the piece of paper, and then turned the page until he saw her picture. An unanticipated shot, he thought, LaRae looking up from a computer keyboard as if she'd been startled. "Still my scared little rabbit, I see." Her hair, lighter in color than he remembered, pulled back with a few escaping strands hanging around her face, showed fine features with adolescents well behind her.

"Do you really think you can leave me?" He knew it was an unreasonable question, but the question echoed painfully in his mind.

"You are my wife and always will be! I don't care what the judge said"; he could not let her go.

Angrily he shouted, "I gave you everything. Don't you know no one denies or challenges me and gets away with it?" Beads of sweat popped out on his forehead as he clenched the clipping into a tight wad in his hand and flung it across the room.

*

LaRae, while staring into the fire snuggled down into the large pillows on her bed. After a short time she could feel her muscles relaxing and the tension leaving her body. Her eyelids become too heavy to hold open. Soon the warmth from the fire and the relaxed condition of her body had her drifting off to sleep.

Awaking to the aroma of fresh perked coffee and bacon sizzling from the kitchen below, she shook off the slumber feeling that tried to lure her back to sleep. Surprised over sleeping more than her usual two hours, she wrapped her robe about her and followed the enticing aroma to the kitchen.

"Morning." LaRae responded between yawns.

She picked up a coffee cup from the drain board and looked about for the coffee pot.

"What's your plan for the day?" Cindy asked.

After LaRae filled the cup with the dark, steaming liquid and settled into a chair, Cindy looked to her for a response.

LaRae took a sip from the cup before answering.

"I thought I would check in with the company to make sure everything is still on with the assignment and that nothing has come up to change the plans."

Cindy no longer able to hide her concern for her friend responded,

"You just arrived last night. There will be plenty of time for work. You need to take some time for yourself and for us to catch up."

LaRae, noting the look of concern on her friend's face slowly sipped from the cup in her hands, before responding to her friend's plea. Cindy's attention was momentarily drawn back to the skillet on the stove where the bacon sizzled. LaRae considered Cindy's words.

"Maybe you're right. I'll check in with the company in a few days"

She mustered a smile and took the plate of eggs, bacon, and toast Cindy handed across the table and placed in front of her.

"I have got to snap out of it," LaRae said to herself, or Cindy will have me in counseling. The episode with the white sedan shook her up more then she realized.

A few days later, LaRae awoke just after seven-thirty and continued to lie in bed for several minutes, listening to the unusual harmony of birds outside her window. She was thoroughly enjoying the serene country atmosphere and her time with Cindy. Throwing back the coverlet and climbing out of bed, and making a quick stop in the bathroom, she opened the bedroom door expecting to hear Cindy clamoring around in the kitchen. One quick sniff proved her expectation overly optimistic.

LaRae walked back to the closet to find her robe. The hardwood floors were cool against her bare feet. A quick glance in the mirror on the back of the door displayed a childlike face, surrounded by loosely tangled hair centered with large sleepy eyes. This would have normally made her look closer to a woman in her twenties rather than her thirties if it wasn't for the dark circles under them. Pulling on the knee-length satin robe over the matching mint green nightgown, she headed down the stairs toward the kitchen.

LaRae entered the kitchen with only one thing on her mind, and that was coffee. After filling the glass pot with water and turning on the switch, LaRae, knowing Cindy would be awakening soon, retrieved two cups from the cup holder displayed on the cabinet near the coffee pot. In a few minutes the aroma of fresh perked coffee filled the kitchen. LaRae inhaled deeply. She loved the smell of fresh perked coffee. The smell would always carry her back into a former time, but unlike other parts of her past these were segments she cherished, segments she didn't get to visit very often because of the nightmares.

LaRae inhaled deeply from the cup she held in her hand and closed her eyes and let the aroma take her back in time. She let her thoughts drift back to a time of wonderful memories, a time before James. Wanting to linger even longer in her memories, she inhaled deeply yet again.

LaRae could see her beloved grandmother—known throughout the countryside for the best biscuits around—up before the break of dawn bustling about the old farmhouse kitchen preparing breakfast. The aroma of coffee saturating the air. LaRae sitting sleepily in grandpa's big rocker; her feet dangling in front of the open fireplace with one of Grandma's handmade quilts wrapped loosely about her; watching the back door for Grandpa to enter with a bucket of fresh milk in his hand.

LaRae's wonderful excursion into yesteryear was suddenly interrupted.

"Morning, this smells so good." Cindy held the fresh brewed coffee up to her nose before taking a sip.

"Yes, I love the smell of fresh coffee."

Cindy, noticing the two pieces of buttered toast on a saucer in front of LaRae made a comment. "Nourishing breakfast."

"I wasn't very hungry this morning." Wanting to stop any conversation geared toward her lack of appetite and lack of sleep, LaRae quickly changed the subject. "What are your plans for the day?"

"Nothing for the day," Cindy paused. "You remember I told you about the fund raiser for the Children's Hospital? The Benefit Masquerade Ball."

LaRae made a questionable frown.

"I know I told you about it, because you told me at the time you didn't know for sure if you would be here or not."

LaRae definitely remembered she was trying hard to think of some way to get out of it.

"It's tonight and you're here."

"I didn't bring any formal attire with me so I'll just hang around at home while you go. It won't bother me at all."

"No way, I know this charming shop in town that will have just what you'll need." Cindy noticing a frown on LaRae's face hurried to try and change her friend's mind. "You know we haven't been anywhere together except at this ranch since you got here. Besides a night out on the town could prove to be good for you." Seeing that LaRae was still not persuaded, Cindy continued to plead with her. "Come on, you'll be with me, of course you'll have fun."

All LaRae could think about was, "I'll be in a strange place, around strange people. There will be cameras there that I'll have to try and avoid. I'll have to remember to never remove my mask." LaRae picked the dishes up from the table and stacked them in the sink before answering Cindy. "Will you stay close to me, and when I'm ready to leave can we leave?"

Cindy seeing the fear on her friends face shook her head affirmatively, and answered. "Yes, whatever you want."

With their shopping completed and a light supper concluded, the two women concentrated on preparing themselves for the evening ahead of them. While Cindy was having a hard time making up her mind on which outfit to wear, LaRae was lingering a little longer in a tub of bubble bath that permeated the air with the aroma of white orchids.

After lengthy consideration, Cindy's final decision, well thought-out, was an emerald green satin midi length sheath. Since the dress was sleeveless she would top it with a gold brocade bolero jacket. The accessories chosen were a green and gold small satin handbag, matching green satin pumps, a gold chain belt, and she would layer several different lengths of gold chains around her neck. The gold mask she picked out would set off her wardrobe perfectly.

LaRae wore backless sapphire blue chiffon, above the knee, length gown, which was slightly gathered at the waist. The blue of the gown set off her porcelain complexion and blue eyes to perfection. Her blond hair was piled atop her head with tiny curls pulled out to frame her face, a style that gave an impression of profound femininity to her looks. She selected a silver lace shawl to match the strapless pumps and a small evening bag. The only jewelry she wore was a sapphire and diamond ring, which was a birthday gift, on her sixteenth birthday, from her now deceased, beloved grandmother.

Two hours later, looking and feeling good, the two women entered the building where the masquerade ball was being held. Not long after entering the plush establishment, LaRae was having second thoughts about letting Cindy talk her into coming. For one thing, Nathan and Carla Brock, the hosts, had been looking forward to meeting her, according to Cindy. Carla's greeting of her was cordial enough, but Nathan's was a bit over done. He gave her a wet kiss of greeting that would have landed on her lips if she hadn't turned her head in time. Then, looped a large plump arm around her waist and spent the next five minutes breathing liquored breath in her face while twirling her around the crowded dance floor.

By eleven o'clock, both dance floors, located at either end of the huge building, were so crowded that one could hardly move an inch, much less dance. Cindy kept urging her out on the floor each time a gentleman would ask.

"Go on Darling, have a good time. Mingle, socialize." She would say.

LaRae tried.

"Hell-o."

LaRae looked up into the face of a man whom was one of her recent dance partners. She could not remember his name but she could remember dancing with him earlier in the evening.

"You looked thirsty, so I came on a mission of mercy."

He held out a flute of champagne in his outstretched hand.

"Thank you." LaRae said, as she took the glass and sipped at the bubbling liquid inside of it. Immediately the young man at her side launched into a discussion on the differences between his construction company compared to others of the same type. He seemed determined to occupy her time with continuous talk of large companies and who's who in each company. Smiling as best she could, and trying to look interested she suppressed at yawn. Suddenly, she felt that familiar sensation, which made the hair on the back of her neck stand up. She was immediately on alert and searching for something to hid behind to conceal herself.

"Will you please excuse me? I need to talk to Cindy about something." She said politely, and before the young man could respond she slipped past him and made her way through the crowd toward her friend.

Someone was watching her. She knew it; she could feel their eyes on her. The strange feeling came again. This was silly and she knew it, especially in a room this crowded. It's almost impossible to look past the person standing next to you. Still the feeling of being watched persisted.

LaRae turned slowly as if only shifting her weight, while doing so she scanned the crowed room. She inhaled sharply. Yes, there was someone watching her, a man. He was looking at her sternly the way James always did. Suddenly a woman grasped the man's arm and coaxed him onto the dance floor. The crowd opened as they entered the floor and soon they were in a sea of people that flowed around them swallowing them up.

As inconspicuous as possible, LaRae proceeded toward the open terrace doors. The terrace was only a little less crowded than the interior of the building, but at least the air wasn't as thick. Standing still for several seconds trying to calm her trembling body, she inhaled deeply several times and then gave a little laugh.

Noticing some stone steps that led from the terrace to the gardens below, LaRae walked in that direction. A winding path took her from the noisy confusion of the crowd past flowering shrubs and heavily laden rose bushes. Soon her steps slowed and she removed her mask. She breathed in deeply the intoxicating aroma of the mixture of the flowers and shrubbery

For an instant, she thought she was being followed. She paused, lifted and half turned her head, listening, trying to sense a presence.

Questions, all at once, run through LaRae's mind.

"Was she being followed by the man she'd seen watching her? Had she been careless coming out here by herself? Had she at any time removed her mask inside the building?"

LaRae came upon a stonewall marking the end of the path. Hearing a noise behind her, she whirled around just in time to bump directly into the man who'd been watching her earlier. He stood before her blocking her escape back up the path from which she had just come.

"What are you doing here?" She asked still shaken by his presence.

He smiled arrogantly. "Enjoying the view, the same as you. Do you object to that?"

A flush rose in her cheeks. "Why should I? It is a public place."

He wore a pasted-on smile, yet his eyes never left her face. He was making LaRae nervous, so she drew herself up to all of her five-foot height and gave him her coolest look.

"Excuse me."

His eyebrows shot up instantly.

"Yes?"

"Would you please step aside? I would like to return now."

He took a step forward. His body, no longer in the shadows, glowed from the moonlight. His six-foot frame with its powerful chest and strong muscled arms caught LaRae's attention. He could easily overpower her.

The sound of his voice brought her out of her thoughts back to reality. His voice was low pitched and firm with conviction.

"Sure, LaRae. I have a question for you first."

He reached out as she tried to dart past him his hand closing around her bare upper arm for only a moment before she was able to shake loose from his grip and continue up the path, never once looking back to see if he was following her.

After reaching the safety of the terrace, LaRae paused, before going through the doors, to compose herself. Entering the main building, she searched through the crowd to locate Cindy. Spotting her in the middle of a small group of people, in deep conversation with one of the woman, LaRae headed in that direction.

A look of apprehension covered Cindy's face when she noticed LaRae approaching the group. Not wanting the group to hear the conversation between her and LaRae she excused herself and walked to meet her.

"Where have you been? What happen to you?"

LaRae tried to calm the trembling in her voice before she spoke, but without success. "We need to go now!"

Cindy never once questioned her friend's decision. "Of course, immediately. Let's get out of here." Cindy taking her friend by the arm led her to the front of the building. "Wait here for me; I'll go get the truck."

"No…I'll go with you," came LaRae's broken response. She did not want to be left alone.

CHAPTER 3

It had been a little over two weeks since LaRae's arrival in Crosstimber. During that time she'd done as Cindy had suggested. She had taken time for herself. LaRae had been sleeping in; awaking long after Cindy left for work, spending her days relaxing, by taking short walks, and reading some of the books she had never seemed to have the time for before. When Cindy was home the two of them would saddle up horses and take long rides over the property, sometimes camping out along the creek bank for a couple of days, like they use to do when they were younger.

She made sure to never leave the ranch except for the one time she attended the charity ball for the Children's Hospital. Since the incident she encountered there, LaRae had been even more on her guard. Not wanting to put her friend's life in any more danger than she already had, LaRae knew she had to cut her visit with Cindy short.

Knowing her time with her friend would soon be coming to an end, especially after the episode with the stranger at the masquerade ball, she tried to make the most of every day. The longer she stayed; the more risk of James finding her in Crosstimber and making the connection between her and Cindy, therefore putting her friend's life in jeopardy. Even though she was extra cautious since the ball, LaRae realized she could never be cautious enough when it came to dealing with James. Now her problem, figuring out how to tell Cindy.

The phone rang, and LaRae crossed the living room of Cindy's rambling, ranch house and eased down on the couch to answer it.

"Hello."

"Ms. Jones?"

"Yes." LaRae answered cautiously.

"Ms. Jones, my name is Cyrus Townsend." His voice was soft and deep, and even over the phone the force of a strong yet curiously gentle character was evident.

LaRae exhaled, "Yes, Mr. Townsend?"

"Your employer gave this number; I hope you don't mind my calling you on your time off?"

La Rae was instantly put at ease because she knew her employer was the only one she gave Cindy's phone number to for contact.

"I don't mind. What can I do for you, Mr. Townsend?"

"Well Ms. Jones, I'd like to know if you would mind starting your assignment a little earlier than first agreed upon."

"May I ask why?" she asked with reservation.

"As you well know we're setting up a new cardiac care hospital in Southwest Arkansas, and I need a cardiac care instructor, but what you don't know is that our computer programmer up and quit on us at the last minute. When I called you company to delay your assignment and explained to them my predicament, they informed me that you are also a computer programmer. So see, we not only need a cardiac care instructor to set up the unit and train the staff, but also someone to set up the new computer program. Are you interested?" He paused, "I promise you will be well compensated for the double duty."

"Yes," she answered without giving herself time to think how odd the coincidence was. "I'm ready for a new challenge." She responded.

"Excellent, when may I expect you?"

"I'll have to get back with you on the details in a couple of days. Will that be okay?"

"That will be fine. I'll be expecting your call. Goodbye Ms. Jones, we'll be talking to you soon."

"Goodbye Mr. Townsend you'll be hearing from my company in

a couple of days."

She cradled the receiver slowly back in its place and sat gazing at it while she pondered over the conversation she had just had with Cyrus Townsend.

"Arkansas! The answer to my present problem."

What a strange twist, she thought, to be moving to an area of the country she had frequented so often as a child to visit kinfolks. And, she not only would be able to leave Crosstimber so Cindy would be safe, but also she would still be far away from James because he was, no doubt, still in Baltimore—she hoped.

Cindy stirred the fire with the brass poker; she then placed another log in the fireplace. Early autumn had arrived bringing with it chilly evenings.

"I just love the warmth of an evening fire on these autumn evenings, don't you?" Cindy remarked while placing the metal screen back in front of the open fireplace.

LaRae was curled up on the sofa preoccupied with the book she had been reading. "Uh-huh." She answered never looking up from the book she held in front of her.

"I think I'll start supper. Are you hungry?" Cindy asked walking toward the kitchen.

"Uh-huh." LaRae answered as she continued to read.

Cindy stopped to look at LaRae positioned on the sofa, smiling mischievously she said, "There's a giant clown riding on a back of a donkey accompanied by a ten piece band at the door, should I let them in?"

"LaRae never looking up from the book in her hands answered, "Uh-huh," And turned the page.

Cindy could no longer able to hold in the laughter that was bubbling up inside of her. Small quakes of giggling rose to the surface. Unable to contain her amusement, she let out a hardy, loud roaring laugh. Convulsing with laughter, she looses her balance and falls against the wall sliding slowly to the floor. Tears of joy streamed down her cheeks.

LaRae, startled by Cindy's action closed her book, looked curiously at her friend on the floor and asked, "What in the world has gotten into you?" LaRae putting the book on the table and walking over to where Cindy sat on the floor, laughing uncontrollably, sat down beside her.

"You...you...and you're uh-huh." Cindy sputtered between convulsions of laughter.

"What's so funny?" LaRae asked starting to giggle. "It's true. Laughter is contagious." She was trying hard to look offended between spurts of giggles. The two women continued to laugh hysterically for several minutes.

Finally gaining control of herself, Cindy reached for the box of tissues on the table close beside her. Taking a couple out of the box for herself, she then passed the box to LaRae. The two smiled at each other as they wiped tears of laughter from their eyes.

"Laughing makes you thirsty." Cindy said pushing herself up off the floor. "Want something to drink?" She asked over her shoulder on her way to the kitchen. She was overjoyed to hear the laughter coming from her dear friend.

"It also leaves you exhausted." LaRae declared leisurely pushing herself up off the floor.

After eating a scrumptious evening meal, the two women relaxed on big fluffy pillows in front of the radiant warmth of the fireplace. Several minutes of silence passed before LaRae looking at Cindy spoke softly. "The time has come for me to leave." She had been dreading this moment every since receiving the phone call from Mr. Townsend. She knew her departure would be hard on both her and Cindy, but it was best LaRae leave now.

Repositioning herself on the pillows so she could look directly at LaRae Cindy slowly asked. "When?"

"In a couple of days." LaRae then looked around for the book she had been reading earlier. Finding it, she removed a folded piece of paper from between the pages. Carefully unfolding the paper she read aloud. "I have to report to a Mrs. Hatcher at St Peter's Hospital in Arkansas."

"Didn't you use to visit relatives in Arkansas when you were younger?"

"Yes, my Great Aunt Kate, my grandmother's sister, but she passed away years ago."

"Will you have a place to stay?"

"Yes, but I have to contact my attorney and have him take care of some business matters, first." LaRae knew she was deliberately being evasive with her friend.

"You know you are welcome to stay here as long as you like and work at the local hospital—are you sure you want to leave—now?" Cindy could not hide the concern written all over her face.

"Yes, I have to go," LaRae responded softly. "This is my job." LaRae was silent for a few minutes before she spoke again. This time she spoke with assurance. "I'm not sure of a lot of thing concerning my life." She paused and taking a slow deep breath before continuing she said, "There's only one thing I'm sure about right now, and it's my ability in doing what I've been trained to do and knowing I do good quality work."

LaRae looked at the large picture hanging above the fireplace. It was one of Cindy and Nick's wedding pictures. Theirs was truly a fairy tale romance she thought. Everything was beautifully arranged. Nick and Cindy looked like a prince and princess in their wedding attire. Their wedding would have rivaled Prince Charming and Cinderella's. LaRae then let her eyes move slowly down to the smaller picture standing on the mantel of Nick in his military uniform. It was taken shortly before the army jeep he was traveling in overturned taking his life. "When…?"

Cindy noticing what drew LaRae's attention interrupted her question. "I know what you're going to ask before you ask it. The same thing Nick's parents ask every time I go visit them."

"Nick has been dead for almost five years now. LaRae spoke gently. Don't you think it's time to move on with your life?"

"What makes you think I haven't moved on with my life?" Cindy was becoming irritated with her friend. "Just because I don't have a man in my life doesn't mean I don't have a life. What Nick and I had was real, and real love can't be ordered up or bought at your friendly neighborhood market." Cindy looked at her friend in hopes she understood.

"I know that the love you and Nick had between you was real. I never doubted it for a minute. I just worry about you, with your dad dieing of a heart attack two years after you lost Nick and you losing your mom when you where a child," LaRae paused and gave Cindy a looked of concern. "You're all alone now."

"Oh, no, I'm never alone; my heavenly Father promised me He would never leave me nor forsake me. He has been with me through my deepest darkest hours."

LaRae said no more because she never knew how to respond to Cindy's religious talk.

The two women once again lapsed into silence; they were contented to just relax. The peacefulness of the evening never quite reached their thoughts but the warmth of the fire soothed their weary bodies if not their minds.

*

LaRae placed her overnight bag on the floorboard behind the driver's seat and then carried the remaining luggage to the rear of her SUV where she pushed it tightly under the back seat. After several checks to make sure she left nothing behind that could be traced backed to her and many tearful hugs to Cindy, LaRae was once more on the road again.

"On the road again—not even, on the run again!" LaRae sneered at herself as she turned the volume up on her radio. She chose to travel at night stopping only for gas. It made her feel safer. If she felt herself getting tired she would stop at the nearest convenient store where she would splash cool water on her face and purchase a large coffee. During the day she would rent a motel room where she would shower, take short naps of two to three hours, and eat a meal purchased from the nearest fast food restaurant.

Upon arriving in town, LaRae drove slowly following her attorney's directions carefully. This would be the first time to visit this place since coming here with her grandmother when she was a young child. As she came around the final bend of the long driveway, LaRae could hardly believe her eyes. The house was more than a surprise. She didn't know quite what she had expected, but certainly not this beautifully renovated old house perched near the edge of a small hill overlooking the valley below. It was more than seventy-five years old, probably closer to a hundred years old. The house was built of weathered natural stone, in the style vaguely reminiscent of an English cottage, with well-kept grounds and a spectacular view of the valley. It had been built by her Great Uncle Joe's parents and had been given to Aunt Kate and Uncle Joe when they were not long married.

Before LaRae had inherited it the house had been closed up for more than a decade. Aunt Kate, up in age, had moved into a small apartment in town a few years prior to her death. With apparent intentions of moving back in, she had thrown a multitude of workmen into renovating and restoring the old antiquated structure. The results were breathtaking and rendered the house the impressive beauty she was now beholding. Taking in the entire panoramic view from the driveway, LaRae drank in the exquisiteness of a piece of property she now owned through inheritance.

This still left LaRae baffled, since she hardly knew Aunt Kate. She remembered visiting her great aunt often with her grandmother Lois, Aunt Kate's younger sister, during the summer months when she was out of school. After Grandpa William died, LaRae and Grandma Lois would take trips to visit Aunt Kate. But, that was when LaRae was young and she didn't remember a great deal about the trips, she scarcely remembered the house.

The realtor LaRae's attorney had hired to care for the place, as it turned out, had been a very responsible and thoughtful manager as well. She had presented LaRae's attorney with an inventory of the contents of the house as well as the yearly bank statement and an appraisal from the insurance company. The realtor had also hired a grounds keeper to take care of the lawn and gardens, a cleaning woman to take care of the housekeeping, and had been selective about whom she allowed to lease the property.

LaRae certainly had nothing to complain about. She told her lawyer that she wanted all income from the property put into a special account and that she wanted no communication concerning the property ever sent to her home address. All expenses were to be paid out of the estates account. According to the realtor's itemized records, LaRae's wishes had been followed thoroughly. She had all intentions of keeping this property a secret from James in case someday she ever needed someplace to go.

"Well, I guess someday has come," she said to herself.

She didn't understand why Aunt Kate had left the property to a relative that barely knew her. LaRae knew that Grandma Lois and Aunt Kate were very close as sisters, but that still didn't explain Aunt Kate making her the sole heir of an estate that could have been left to closer relatives. The way Aunt Kate had renovated it; restoring the house and grounds; repairing and replacing interior walls and fixtures; and leaving the place ready to be occupied at a moment's notice was somehow prophetic. It was as if she had had a second sense that someday LaRae would have a need to live here and she was making sure everything would be in order for her occupancy. It just didn't make sense!

LaRae spent the first few days familiarizing herself with her house and the grounds. The peacefulness of the countryside and the gorgeous scenic views of the valley below was one of a pure picturesque beauty. Her favorite view was from the terrace or the balcony of her bedroom that overlooked the landscape of the valley below. Nothing compares to the beauty of this scene at sunset with glowing bright colors of orange, red, and yellow flames of fire painted across the evening sky.

The second Monday after her arrival, she made her way into town to St. Peter's Hospital to meet with Cyrus Townsend; the head of the cardiac care unit and Mrs. Hatcher, the supervisor of that unit, to start her new assignment.

Cyrus Townsend was a short, plump, balding man in his mid fifties. He had a continuous smile plastered across his face. The only signs of wrinkles were the laugh lines around the corners of his big bright blue eyes. He was of a jovial nature and LaRae instantly liked him. He introduced her to Mrs. Hatcher who was of a different character altogether. She was of a more serious type, but the calmness in her voice eased any apprehensions LaRae might have had at their greeting. LaRae soon found out that Mrs. Hatcher, being an ex-army nurse was a very detailed person and expected those under her supervision to be just as detailed. She was, in fact, a perfectionist in her job duties and no doubt expected the same of her co-workers. That would be no problem to LaRae because she was a bit of a perfectionist herself.

LaRae was completely at ease in the company of Mr. Townsend and Mrs. Hatcher. Cyrus Townsend, although he took his job seriously, could always find humor in all experiences of life. It wasn't long before he had her laughing at some of the silliest work-related jokes. Mrs. Hatcher, though quite reserved, even cracked a smile at the telling of them. They both inquired about her experience and ability to program the databases in the cardiac care unit with the new program St. Peter's Hospital was being required to put into operation. The impressive resume she provided to them actually spoke for itself. She was more than happy to prove to her new employers her knowledge of computers and nursing skills matched the information presented in her resume.

LaRae spent the rest of that Monday morning with Lorraine Hatcher briefing her on her job duties and introducing her to the rest of the staff she would be working with. They broke for lunch around 12:30 and after eating, Mrs. Hatcher offered LaRae the rest of the day off so she would be refreshed for work first thing the next morning. This would also provide her time to look over the employee manual and familiarize herself with its contents. LaRae accepted her boss's offer and returned to the warmth and comfort of her home.

*

LaRae looked around her new home of six months with appreciation. It astonished her how much Aunt Kate's taste of style and furniture matched her own. She had meticulously sewn the drapes from material she had handpicked to match the distinct shade of paint Aunt Kate had selected for the walls. LaRae remembered the days, after she first arrived, searching used furniture and antique stores for precise pieces of furniture she needed to depict the exact era she wanted. It was wonderful roaming about the big old house and soaking in the peace and charm of its beauty—a beauty she had helped create. She knew her best creative ideas had gone into decorating the place with a style of furniture and coordinating colors that made it uniquely hers.

LaRae awoke with a jolt confused, quivering, and drenched in sweat; some unknown fear seemed to grip at her very being. Her heart was pounding, as she slowly looked around the room terrified to move.

"Why am I so afraid?" she gasped.

She consciously had to take slow deep breaths to slow her rapid breathing. LaRae turned her head slightly to look at the clock on her bedside table when awareness penetrated through the haziness in her mind.

"Ugh two in the morning." she groaned as she set up in the bed.

Knowing she would not go right back to sleep, she threw back the covers and gradually got out of bed, walked to the kitchen, and poured herself a small glass of milk. She then slowly walked through the den and beyond to the sun-porch and curled up on the chaise longue at the end of the porch. LaRae placed the half empty glass on the table beside her and proceeded to reflect on what had awakened her in such a state.

"I had that same dream again." She declared as she remembered it all so clearly.

It seemed to me I stood outside of a residence and my entrance to the pathway beyond was blocked by a large iron gate, weathered with age. There was a tarnished chain wrapped around the gate with a large padlock securing it closed. In this dream I called out to make my presence known and yet, no acknowledgment came and peering closer through the rusted bars of the gate I saw that the home was closed up and neglected.

Then all of a sudden like a spirit I passed through the metal gate before me. As I made my way up the pathway I noticed it was narrow and overgrown with weeds. The trees that once stood fine and tall lining the path and were standing naked in the night death all around them. I peered ahead toward the house, no smoke was seen coming from the still standing chimney and the night was cool. The lattice shutters hung askew around the dark shadowy windows. As I looked upon the house once more I could tell the once charming home stood in ruins, a shadow of what it used to be.

I thought to myself, "What is the meaning of this? Why am I here?"

For it appeared, as I gazed around, that all the plant life seemed yellowed and browned with death, as if it had been blown across by a hot desert wind and the once charming place stood with death all around it. Everywhere I looked all was deteriorating and decaying. Once more as I looked upon the house every once in a while I could see a small little flicker like the small flame of a candle.

Then, I don't know why, some unknown fear seemed to grasp at my very being, and all I could think about was escaping from this dark place.

At that moment, "I woke up." She declared, "Why do I always wake up at that specific time? What's going on?" She questioned while looking upward toward the ceiling.

LaRae was still downstairs relaxing in the chaise on the sun-porch when she noticed lights pass very slowly by on the main road. At night when she looked through the wooded area surrounding the property and beyond, automobile headlights could be seen passing on the main road below, especially now that it was autumn and the leaves of the trees had begin to fall.

Autumn, it has been almost a year since leaving my last assignment in Wyoming, and almost a year since last seeing Cindy. "Oh, how I miss you, my dear friend." LaRae whispered. She knew to make another visit this soon after the last one would only be putting her friend in fatal danger, and she would not take that chance with her friend's life.

Always on guard, LaRae breathed a sigh of relief as she watched the slowly passing headlights travel on down the road. The clock on the mantel in the den chimed four, and she knew it wouldn't be long before the sun would be making its appearance for the day. Picking up the empty milk glass from the table, placing it on the counter top as she passed through the kitchen, turning off all lights downstairs except for the one in the entry hall and returning upstairs to her bedroom, she crawled into bed in hopes of finding the sleep she so desperately needed.

For a few more months, if the past patterns held true, she'd be safe here, at least that long—long enough to finish her extended assignment and move on before James found her secret place. She'd managed over a year at her last assignment before the phone call came which ignited the fear that launched her into packing her belongings sending her away under the cover of darkness. But now here she was in Aunt Kate's house.

"No, my house." LaRae quickly corrected herself. She was in a house that belonged to her; a house that she loved; one that was uniquely hers. But, it—like her—become a target as soon as she made the decision to set up residency in it. She knew the consequences when she made that decision. Her desire to have a stable life and a sense of belonging sometimes overcome her better judgment. Because of this desire, James always managed to get too close.

LaRae remembered how James reacted when she left him the first time. They were still living in an apartment not far from her parent's home. It was after an argument and he had hit her across the face knocking her into a wall. She ran out of the house, barefooted, all the way to her parent's home to see her mother. When he found her, he was all apologetic and promised "never again." His promises never lasted more than a couple of weeks. After her parents found out about his third abusive attack, within two weeks he had them packed-up and moved to Baltimore—away from her family and all her friends. Luckily, Cindy was not in the picture at this time because she had married Nick and moved to Texas with her new husband. With so many of her other friends in her life there was never an occasion to bring Cindy up to James. Therefore, James never knew of Cindy's existence.

Just after the divorce, LaRae moved back to Louisiana and bought a small home just down the road from where her parents lived. She was not able to prove the damage done to that home had been anything other than faulty wiring in an older house, like the fire department had said, but she knew—especially after receiving James' threatening phone call—that he was responsible for its destruction. Losing her home along with everything she owned, and her parent's much-loved dog, Sheba, who died from poisoning, made her realize she could never go near family or friends without putting them in danger. She has been on the run every since.

At first she lived out of her suitcase, in cheap motels in one town after another to keep James from finding her. Eventually, she went back to college and dedicated herself to obtaining a nursing degree. Receiving her degree in nursing, she accepted a position at the local hospital of the town she was living in and started working on her degree in computer science; taking night classes. After completion of her computer science degree, she knew she had to move on. It was to her good fortune she read an advertisement in the local newspaper from a nationwide travel-nursing agency, looking for nurses interested in working and traveling to different locations to work at understaffed hospitals. LaRae felt this was the answer to keeping James from finding her.

However, she completely miscalculated James' relentless effort in pursuing what he considered his. His words became like a broken record in her thoughts as she remembered them all too vividly.

"You can run but you can't hide. I will always find you no matter where you go. I will find you but when I get through with you no one will find you."

A shiver run through her body as his voice echoed through her mind. What frightened her so much was the fact she knew those words were not idle threats. He meant every word then and still does to this very day.

CHAPTER 4

Several days later LaRae was up and out of bed early. She dressed casually in a red sweatshirt and jeans. Since nearing the end of the computer programming part of her assignment, she would be doing the majority of the work on her computer from home. She developed a routine over the last few months. Every morning she would eat a light breakfast, take a stimulating morning jog down the long driveway, and then retreat to her office to work.

The day started out cloudy with threats of rain at the beginning of LaRae's morning walk. On several occasions it seemed the sun and the gray rain clouds were at war with each other. First drizzling rain would fall then the sun would peek through just in time to stop the threatening downpour. The sun victorious, exuberated full control of the sky, shined brightly for all to see.

LaRae walked briskly up the twisting driveway. She sang cheerfully as she put the key in the lock. The phone was ringing as she opened the door. Thinking it could be Cyrus Townsend calling back on the proposal she presented last week she broke into a run to answer it and grabbed the receiver on the third ring.

"Hello." She puffed breathlessly into the receiver.

LaRae's apprehension returned when no one answered her greeting. She knew someone was still on the phone because she heard the even, heavy, breathing on the other end of the line. She almost dropped the phone when a harsh male voice started laughing. After a significant pause, the man said. "You can run but you can't hide."

LaRae dropped the phone receiver to the floor, and reached out a trembling finger to cut off the connection. A sudden feeling of being sick to her stomach overcame her. Running to the bathroom, she then heaved. She rinsed out her mouth, and then gulped a small glass of water. Staggering back into the living room, she weakly dropped onto the sofa, curled up into a ball, and begins to weep uncontrollably.

A little while later, she uncurled from the ball, wiped her face, and then rose to her feet.

"I have to try and get some work done," she murmured, as she slowly walked to her office down the hall.

Refusing to think about the recent phone call anymore, for now at least, she tried to concentrate on the work that was spread out on the table before her. Still getting her thoughts together, she organized different scenarios and diagrams on different colored index cards. She willed her mind to stay on the project and managed to stay occupied for a few minutes, but caught herself glancing out the window several times. Finally, giving in to the restless urge to move about, she walked over to the window nearest her and stood looking out.

Even with the early-morning rain still clinging to some of the tree branches and settling lightly into the low places here and there the view was lovely. The house and yard on the south side was set well back from the hill's edge and the outer boundaries were surrounded with woods. The sloping ground had been divided into several tiered gardens with a lightly wooded area beyond. Nearest the house was a flagstone terrace with hand carved wooden tables and chairs, flanked on each side of the steps were heavy stone planters filled with flowering plants that clung to the last of their fall blossoms.

Without being aware of it, she lifted a hand and placed it against the cool glass of the windowpane as she gazed out. She loved the natural beauty of this area. A sense of motion caught her attention, and she watched as a rabbit crept across the lawn beyond the terrace toward the wooded area. LaRae felt a jolt as she recognized the expression on her face reflected in the glass pane.

It was a look of fear. She was afraid. The fear had more than one level, like steps going down into pure darkness, and she couldn't make herself move from that spot. She stood in front of the windows, shaken by her own image, and frozen by memories of past torments. Because she could feel the danger that constantly lurked in the shadows all about her, she couldn't forget the pain and helplessness that James had taught her, and couldn't make herself believe her life would ever be any different.

Getting her trembling body under control, she walked back to her desk and started neatly packing all her work for the current assignment into a large plastic container. Completing the task, she reluctantly picked up the receiver of the phone on her desk. Knowing what she had to do, she dialed the number to her local realtor to inform her that the home would be available yet again for leasing. Then she put in a call to Cyrus Townsend and told him she would be leaving her position with St. Peter's a week early to take on another assignment.

Once more LaRae knew she had to run. As much as she loved her home and felt for the first time she really belonged somewhere, she had to pack and leave. She had to once more go into hiding! She could not let James find her here in her secret place. In addition to killing her, knowing how much this place means to her, he would destroy her sanctuary and make her watch. She could not allow that to happen.

LaRae wasted no time packing up her personal belongings and making arrangements with the realtor to place the items she had left behind into a local storage unit. She then contacted her attorney to make preparations to pay for the storage unit out of the profits from the property. Within two days LaRae was out of her home and checked into a local bed and breakfast under an alias, located a town away from the home Aunt Kate had given her.

*

Gilbert Garth opened the large brown envelope that his secretary had placed on his desk earlier that morning. He noticed there was no return address on the outside of the package. After flipping through each newspaper clipping and article of papers, Gilbert let out a slow whistle. According to the items that were contained in the envelope, LaRae Jones and James Ashcroft had been married for a short time. LaRae Jones had gotten an uncontested divorce and had taken back her maiden name. According to the court documents she hadn't accepted any settlement or alimony, and there had been no children of the marriage.

"So why was I hired by the ex-husband to find Ms. Jones?"

According to what he just read, the man had no reason to harass the woman, not financially, anyway. After reviewing the documents several times, Gilbert knew he had to consider other possibilities in this case before giving Mr. Ashcroft any more information.

*

Always vigilant, LaRae never departed or returned to the *Bed and Breakfast*, where she now resided, the same way more than twice. She, placing her blue SUB into storage, now traveled about in a small economy car she bought and licensed under alias name.

LaRae hardly recognized herself s she gazed at her reflection in the rearview mirror. Her own long platinum blond hair was now replaced with light ginger colored chin length hair. And, her light sapphire eyes are now deep emerald-green, thanks to contacts. Not only did she trade her silks and satins for denim and cotton, but also her heels and pumps for boots and tennis. LaRae took great pains to transform herself from the big city rich businessman's wife to a hard working small town country girl.

"Goodbye LaRae Jones and hello Nancy Carter," LaRae said after taking one last look in her rearview mirror.

Slipping in through the back door of *Country Living Bed & Breakfast*, LaRae made her way through to the Kitchen where she found Shirley, the proprietor, making preparations for the morning meal. "Good morning," Nancy said upon seeing her standing over the sink.

"Mornin, you're up early," Shirley responded after placing the pot she had just filled with water on the stove.

"Earlier than usual," Nancy answered as she took the hot steaming cup of coffee from the proprietor and sat at the small kitchen table to the left of the prep-bar.

"Couldn't you sleep?" Shirley asked with a look of motherly concern on her face.

"I don't usually sleep more than five or six hours, and I went to bed early." LaRae didn't want to let Shirley know she was a restless sleeper and never got more than two or three hours sleep a night. "I had a large cup of coffee in your flower garden while I watched the sun rise. You do have beautiful sunrises here"

Nancy watched Shirley as she expertly went about with the preparation for the morning meal. Shirley, a widow for several years, appeared to be in her early sixties and stood at a height of approximately five feet seven inches tall. She was plump around the middle, most likely from enjoying too many of her own delicious meals. The woman did love to cook. Except for the few curly locks hanging loosely about the face, her salt and pepper hair was neatly twisted up into some type of a bun that sat low on the back of her head. She was always humming or singing softly as she went about her work, as she was doing now.

"Nancy Carter you are a mysterious one." Shirley stated looking at her all of a sudden.

LaRae wincing at the use of her alias, asked, "How?"

"You're a young woman yet you avoid any social gatherings even here in the house with the other guest. And you keep your cards close to your chest"

"What do you mean by that?"

"No one knows anything about you, especially me, and I usually know just about everything about everybody." Shirley laughed playfully. "All I know about you is that you came from up north, Wisconsin I think you said, and about three weeks ago you finished up your assignment at the hospital."

"What were you singing," LaRae asked trying to change the subject.

"Oh, just one of my favorite hymns, Amazing Grace."

LaRae looked at her curiously.

Noticing the strange look on Nancy's face, Shirley replied, "I take it you don't know the song. It's a song about my savior who died for me."

"Oh, it's one of those God things."

"Nancy do you not know about Jesus and what he did for you?" Shirley softly asked with sincere caring in her voice.

"Yes, of course, he was born in a manger to the Virgin Mary and her husband Joseph around Christmas time, and the three wise men brought gifts. When I was young, my Grandmother used to take me every Christmas to see the program at her church." Nancy answered defensively.

"But do you know him?"

"Does anyone really know God? Besides I need you to explain to me how knowing a God that is supposed to be good and loving would turn His back on me and allow terrible things to happen to me and in my life, is suppose to be a good thing?" Forgetting herself for a moment she spouted forth words of pain that had been hidden deep in her subconscious.

With tears in her eyes and wanting to avoid anymore conversation along these lines, Nancy, respectfully got up from her chair, placed her empty cup in the sink, and continued into the entryway and up the stairs to her rooms.

Shirley was taken aback, surprised by the admittance, and stunned by the truth she saw in Nancy's eyes. This young woman's emerald green eyes were wide open, laid bare for inspection. The shame, private agony, and terror Shirley saw there affected her deeply. It hurt to witness this young woman's pain. This girl was seriously terrified of someone or something and was on the run.

As Nancy closed the heavy door behind her, with tears flowing from her eyes, she leaned against it and slid down it to the floor. For the first time in years, Nancy wished that she had someone to turn to, someone to confide in. Not Shirley though. She didn't want her to know about it, didn't want her to see the shame and constant fear she bore. If Shirley knew everything, that knowledge might make her think less of Nancy, and she could not handle seeing the disapproval in her new friend's eyes.

Nancy stood up as she heard the light knock on the door of her room, and wasn't surprised when Shirley poked her head in. But, she was surprised to realize that it was dark outside and to see a tray in her landlord's hands.

"It's after seven and you didn't come down for lunch or supper," she said. "I cooked fried chicken. Do you think you could eat a little?" She asked as she placed the tray on a table beside the bed.

Despite herself, Nancy had to smile. "Yes thank you very much," she said.

"When you're ready to talk I'm hear to listen." Shirley tenderly reassured her, as she quietly closed the door leaving Nancy to her meal.

That was what Nancy dreaded. The talking. Reopening old wounds and feelings would only bring back the pain. All the questions she would no doubt ask about the past and the answers Nancy didn't want to give her would only add to the mystery Shirley found in her. She didn't want to go there. She didn't want to relive the fear and shame, and see the look of disapproval on Shirley's face. Nancy believed that look would hurt the most; because in the short time she has been living in Shirley's home she developed a great attachment for the loving woman.

The next few days passed quietly. Nancy with her assignment

completed spent most of her days taking long walks about the grounds of the bed and breakfast and relaxing in Shirley's gorgeous fall gardens with a good book. Yet, she felt like she was in some kind of limbo. It was as if she were waiting for something to happen, like the quite before the storm. Then it happened.

Nancy woke during the late hours of the night, with a scream trapped in her throat. She was setting up in bed, shaking, and the terrifying images of the recurring dream vivid in her mind. The back of her hair wet against her neck, the nightgown she had dawned just hours before soaked and clinging to her body.

After changing her nightgown, Nancy wasn't ready to go back to sleep. She slipped from the bed and, without bothering to turn on a light, went to her door and opened it silently. As soon as she stepped out into the hall, she saw the faint glow of the light in the entryway.

In sock feet she slipped past the closed doors of the other guests and continued down the hall. She went downstairs, winding her way through the house until ending up on the screened in back porch just off the kitchen. Light from the full moon was shining into the room, and there was something welcoming about the white wicker furniture glowing faintly in the center of the room.

She curled up on the nearest chaise, looking out at the twinkling stars without really seeing them. Thoughts swirled around and around in her head. She was in a kind of undefined state, because James was still out there somewhere and a part of her was constantly waiting for him to make a move. Her reality was though he was not here; he still maintained control over her. The great possibility of danger lurking around every corner for her was real.

Nancy closed her eyes tightly as she tried to push the memories away. They were cruel intrusions, an inescapable reminder of the wounds James had left her with; she could feel the lump of anxiety inside her growing larger as she struggled to overcome it. She willed her mind to think of anything except James and soon she was relaxed and comfortable. Within a few minutes she was aware of heavy eyelids and an almost irresistible urge to snuggle down into the overstuffed cushions and the warm blanketed throw to reclaim stolen sleep. She knew she should go back upstairs to her bed, but she couldn't find the will power to move from that spot.

*

It was early morning. James Ashcroft was up and pacing the floor with the phone clenched tightly in his hand and pressed hard against his ear. "Find her, and find her now!" He demanded. "I don't want to hear any excuses!" He continued to pace the floor, anger etched across the drawn crevices in his forehead. "No, Garth doesn't work for me anymore! He wasn't any good anyway. He never came up with any information." James was practically yelling by this time into the phone. "If you want to continue having a job, you had better find those photographs, too, that her attorney threatened to use against me in court."

It was obvious the person on the other end of the phone was not having much input into this conversation. James words were coming too fast and furious for anyone to make much of a response. With final orders again demanding her to be found, James slammed the phone down.

Continuing his pacing back and forth across the living room floor, anger consuming him, he picked up a glass vase from an end table next to the sofa sending it flying across the room at the portrait hanging over the fireplace. It landed dead center of the face of the women painted on the canvass. He was enraged over his unsuccessful efforts to find LaRae and bring her back home where she belonged.

His face was red as crimson; his jaw hard as granite; he looked at the face in the portrait that now was marred by the damage the vase has cut across the center of it and pointed a finger. Sheer rage boiling over, he yelled.

"How dare you leave me—after all I have done for you—I *will* find you and bring you back home—you *are* my wife—I don't care what any judge says!"

He starts to leave the room and with sudden remembrance walks over the desk in the corner. Opening the bottom drawer, he pulls out a package; satisfied the contents where still there, he looks at the portrait on the wall once more and said, "You can run, but you can't hide. I will find you."

*

LaRae roused from her slumber on the chaise, stretched her arms and took note of the sun peaking through the treetops. It was early morning and at first she heard no other sounds except for the wind rustling through the trees. Then, she heard the familiar singing of Shirley coming from the kitchen. Not wanting to be found on the screened-in back porch in only a nightgown, she quietly got up from the comfort of the lounger and before she could make an exit, Shirley came through the kitchen door holding two cups of coffee.

"Good morning," she said with a smile.

"Oh—morning, I didn't know anyone else was up, yet."

Shirley handed LaRae a steaming cup of coffee flavored to her taste with just the right amount of cream and sugar before taking a seat.

Taking the cup from Shirley's hand, LaRae sat back down in the comfort of the seat she had just risen from.

"Is your bed not comfortable?" Shirley inquired. "We can get you another one if you like."

"Oh no—my bed is very comfortable. I just woke early and came down to take in an early sunrise. I was intending to be back in my room before anyone else awoke, but I guess I fell asleep."

Shirley nodded in understanding and then asked. "Is there anything special you'd like for breakfast?"

"Anything you cook is fine with me, it's all good—especially your fluffy biscuits."

Smiling at the genuine compliment the young women made of her expertise in the kitchen; Shirley looked at her watch and informed LaRae the other guest would be coming down for breakfast soon. "If you don't want to get caught in your nighty, you might want to go change."

LaRae jumps up and heads upstairs to dress for the day. She never wanted to miss out on any of Shirley's delicious meals. On her way through the kitchen, she put her coffee cup in the sink to be washed later.

Rummaging through her closet, she picks out a pair of blue jeans with a blue and gray plaid flannel shirt and a gray turtleneck to wear underneath. She wore dark gray ankle high boots with solid square one inch heels. Running a brush quickly through her ginger colored hair, she exited the room and made her way to the dining area joining the other guest.

The conversation around the table was normally lighthearted enough. Once in a while LaRae would be asked for her input about some news article in the local paper or the best restaurant in the area. Of course, the *Country Living Bed & Breakfast* was the best to her hands down. On political issues, LaRae had no interest in politics or politicians at all. As far as she was concerned, all politicians were interested in was winning. Most had no real concerns for the people that voted them into office. LaRae's life with James formed the opinion she now held on this subject. With his money and power, she had seen him manipulate everything and everyone to control all situations in his interest.

One by one the guest finished their meal and left for their planned activities. LaRae followed their lead by going to her room, retrieved a half-read book and walked to the gazebo to sit in the quietness of the garden to be alone. She down in her favorite spot and opened her book. She couldn't concentrate on the words spread across the pages before her. Her mind wanted to drift back to the past. Oh, how she wished she had no past. Sometimes she thought amnesia would be the answer. That way the horrors of the past could never invade her thoughts.

Her attention was drawn to the movement of a small red squirrel scampering along a tree branch hanging near the roof of the gazebo. She watched the little creature run down the tree to the ground and pick up one of the many acorns scattered all about the base of the tree, then quickly scurry back up to its nest, no doubt, obscured from view somewhere within. LaRae was intermittently amused by the playful antics the squirrel displayed as her thoughts bounced back and forth from the past to the present.

Finally giving up on the useless effort to complete the book at hand, she left the gazebo and walked back to her assigned room for a short nap before lunch. Entering the room, she softly closed the door behind her. She eased down on the bed and laid crossways of it, and then grabbed the brightly colored throw folded neatly at the foot and placed it over her.

LaRae was crouched behind a big oak tree hoping James would pass her by and not find her. She was out of breath from running and she knew he was close behind. Looking around from where she was crouching she saw a large iron weathered gate. There was a tarnished chain wrapped around the gate with a large padlock securing the way beyond closed. She crept over to the gate and peered through the rusted bars and saw a house that was long abandoned.

Then all of a sudden she passed like a spirit through the bars of the gate before her. The walkway twisted and turned. Feeling the urge to hurry along the pathway, she made her way toward the house. She noticed it was narrow and overgrown with weeds. Hearing a sound, she glanced behind and James could be seen making his way up the path after her.

Quickening her steps, she peered ahead toward the house. No smoke was seen coming from the chimney and the night was cool. The lattice shutters hung askew around the dark shadowy windows. As she looked upon the house once more she could tell the once charming home stood in ruins, a shadow of what it once use to be.

The sound of footsteps was getting closer. She took off running toward the house through the plant life yellowed and browned with death. Everywhere she looked all was deteriorating and decaying. Once more as she looked upon the house every once in a while she could see a small little flicker of light like the small flame of a candle. "I've got to get away.... I've got to get away.... I've got to get away..."

Fitfully, LaRae aroused from sleep struggling for breath and flung the throw off of her wet drenched body. "That same dream again, she gasped. But this time James was there." She sat up on the side of the bed and took slow deep breaths to calm her rapid heartbeat. Walking to the closet, she selected a change of clothing and headed for the bathroom where in privacy she removed the ginger colored wig. Turning the water on in the shower she adjusted the temperature, and then took off her sweat drenched clothes.

Donning a pair of black slacks and a royal blue sweater, LaRae was ready for supper. She retrieved an identical ginger colored wig from the back of the closet. Pinning her own long blond hair under the stockinet she adjusted the wig fittingly over her head and left the room. Carefully she made her way down the stairs and past the dining area so as not to be noticed. Slipping out the back door she headed toward the garage to her car. Buckling the seat belt, she backed down the driveway and eased the vehicle into the street. Heading in the direction of town, she breathed a sigh of relief knowing she had evaded the police officer that frequented the *Bed & Breakfast* most every evening. Not that she disliked him—she didn't even know him. It is just that she didn't trust people in authority—because of the way they treated her when she desperately needed their help—during the times James beat her so badly she required medical attention.

She crossed a couple of railroad tracks before she arrived at the local diner she normally visited this time of day for her evening meal. She ordered her food to go and then continued to the park where she could be alone to eat. The peace and solace of the area was comforting to her soul as she enjoyed her meal and watched nature in its purest form.

CHAPTER 5

Gilbert Garth scowled as he stood in the concealing shadows of the large shrubs and bushes just outside the boundaries of the Ashcroft's property. Letting the binoculars fall loosely around his neck, he looked around about him to make sure he wasn't discovered lurking about. He had been at this game too long to allow himself to be caught doing his job—a job that consisted of watching others without their knowledge. At first he had felt a bit uncomfortable watching his former employer, but something just didn't add up.

He wasn't working for James Ashcroft, anymore. The morning his former employer had arrived at the investigator's office and heard there was no new information on LaRae Jones; Gilbert received his final pay with a brisk "thank you for all your trouble," and an "I don't need you anymore."

Yet, despite that fact, he was still nagged by the feeling that something was wrong. He wasn't one to allow himself to get attached to a case but there was just something about this one that didn't add up. There was something about the woman, LaRae Jones, which nagged at him. No matter how hard he tried he couldn't let this one go until he had some answers for himself.

He knew LaRae Jones was running from something or some one. He was sure of it. "The lady is afraid of something, I'd bet my pension on it if I had one." He had a habit of thinking out loud. He believed that the possibility of some kind of physical attack was evident with her. She had a kind of animal instinct of self-preservation about her. And having seen the scarcely controlled rage of his former employer on several occasions he was beginning to believe that the someone was Mr. Ashcroft himself.

Remembering the information he had received from another associate in an unmarked envelope, as requested, a few days ago and after pouring over the information, Gilbert came to the conclusion that Mr. Ashcroft needed looking into. He had worked enough domestic cases to figure it was the ex-husband that kept this woman running— and—running scared. The only thing he was still having trouble with was coming up with a motive. LaRae hadn't demanded or accepted one dime from the man. And, he was a wealthy man, who owned a very profitable business.

The private investigator brought the binoculars up to his eyes again and located Ashcroft once more. Gilbert watched as he moved about the living room of the house. James looked both worried and miserable. The phone must have rang because he watched as Ashcroft jerked it up to his ear and shout something into the receiver several times before slamming it back down on the cradle. He picked up something from a nearby table and threw it across the room. At this distance—even with binoculars—it was difficult to determine what he threw. He definitely was in a rage, Gilbert thought. James started to leave the area but must of changed his mind; he then walked to a desk in the corner and retrieved something from inside. He pointed his finger to the other side of the room where he had just thrown the object and was shouting something. "I wish I could hear what he was saying," Gilbert said. "If I could only hear what he saying, maybe the mystery of Mr. Ashcroft would be cleared up."

*

Entering the screened-in back porch, Shirley walked over to where Nancy was stretched out on a lounger reading and handed her one of the two cups of tea she had prepared for them.

"You look like you could use something warm to drink." She said as she pulled up a chair across from Nancy.

"Thank you" Nancy sighed graciously as she placed the book she was reading in her lap.

"What's wrong?" Nancy asked, noticing the concern on Shirley's face.

"We need to talk Nancy. I need you to be honest with me." Shirley spoke softly. As she watched apprehension building in the youthful eyes of the woman across from her, she reached out to gently take hold of Nancy's hand.

"As you know Tuesdays are usually my market day and while I was shopping I noticed a man passing out fliers and asking, 'do you know this woman'?" Shirley paused, reached into the pocket of her jacket, pulled out a folded piece of paper, and handed it to Nancy before continuing.

"The woman in the picture resembles you, except she has long blond hair and blue eyes. Her name is LaRae Jones Ashcroft." Shirley noted the obvious fear on the young woman's face upon hearing those words.

Nancy jumped from the chair, the book she had been reading falling to the ground, and bolted into the house.

With fear clearly having its grip on her, Nancy pulled her luggage from the top of the closet, and positioned the pieces on the bed. She frantically moved between the closet, the bureau, and the dresser, pulling clothing and other personal items out of each and flinging them toward the cases on the bed.

A soft knock sounded on the door before it gentle opened allowing Shirley to enter.

"What are you doing?" Shirley asked seeing Nancy recklessly throwing clothing out of the closet.

"I've got to get out of here! I've got to get out of here!" Nancy exclaimed never once stopping to look at the woman.

"No, LaRae!"

LaRae jumped at the use of her real name and turned to look upon the woman she had grown to love.

"It's time you stop running," Shirley tenderly stated as she took LaRae's hands and gently pulled her to the chair to sit down.

LaRae moaned, "No, you don't understand. I have to get out of here! The longer I stay here the sooner it will be that I'll be found; if I'm found here then I put you and your guest in danger. I don't want that to happen to you."

"What are you running from?"

LaRae felt the pressure of hot tears behind her eyes, and her throat was aching. "My ex-husband, James Ashcroft."

Shirley half nodded, as if she expected that response. "Why?"

LaRae looked down at her feet. "Because he wants to kill me."

Slowly, Shirley took LaRae's hands gently in hers, and then looked at her, waiting until LaRae eyes met her gaze. "He threatened to do that?"

She nodded, answering the next question before it could be asked. "And I believe him. He isn't one to make idle threats."

Shirley frowning, "Did you go to the police?"

LaRae laughed scornfully, "in three different towns. But they can't arrest someone for threats, and I can't prove he would do anything more. My word against his, and he is very good at swaying people to his side. In one town they actually told me I didn't want to have him arrested because it would only make him madder—even though I sat before them with my eyes half swollen shut, bruised, bleeding from my mouth and my cloths ripped and torn! That's the kind of help I got from the police!"

"Why does he want to hurt you?" Shirley didn't doubt one bit that she was telling the truth.

"You have to understand I need to just get out of here," LaRae cried as she jumped up to continue her packing.

"LaRae, why does he want to hurt you?"

LaRae looked away from her, turning her gaze to the door and spoke in an even toned voice. "Because I left him. It was a big blow to his ego." LaRae took a deep breath before continuing, "And because I made him give me a divorce. He hates loosing to anyone, and worse he hates being forced to do something he doesn't want to do."

Looking at the petite woman standing before her and curiosity getting the better of her, Shirley asked, "How did you *make* him give you a divorce?"

"I had photographs of the bruises, doctor's reports, and tapes of the beating administered to me by James. My attorney threatened to use them against him in court." LaRae shuttered at the remembrance of the days in court and then continued. "James didn't need the publicity at the time because of a huge business deal he was trying to close with the city of Baltimore."

"Baltimore!" Shirley exclaimed. "I thought you said you were from Wisconsin!"

"I'm sorry I lied to you. But you have to understand the type of man I've been running from." LaRae looked at Shirley before continuing, "He likes power and he lost some of it when the judge gave me the divorce. I was his wife, his property like a piece of furniture or a car, and his property was taken away from him and he wants it back."

"So you've been running every since."

"It seems to be the only answer. At first I thought he'd get tired of chasing me and just give up, but not now, not after this long. Sometimes months would go by but not much longer than a year before I would see one of his associates outside of my home or place of work, or pick up the phone and hear a strange voice on the other end, hauntingly always reminding me *I can run but I can't hide*."

Despite her even voice and inexpressive face, Shirley knew LaRae was deeply afraid of her ex-husband, and she clearly believed in the man's threats. It was obvious to Shirley this was a powerful man that was use to having his own way and was not going to be told no.

"LaRae, do you not have any family that can help you through this troubling time?" Shirley tried to constrain the anger in her voice, when she saw LaRae cringe from the harshness of the sound of her voice. She watched as the young woman's face turned pale and her eyes widen as she stared blindly at the wall. Though LaRae didn't move a muscle, Shirley had the vivid impression that she was drawing into herself, as if some protective barrier had rose up and was trying desperately to hide her away.

The mention of her family did indeed bring a protective shield around about her. The thought of her parents or her friends being in danger of their lives because of her sent chills throughout her body.

"I don't want to talk about it." Her voice came in small gasps.

"Did James threaten your family too?"

She flinched again, at the sound of the name that meant only pain and terror. Then, slowly, Shirley saw the reflection of a private hell in LaRae's wide emerald green eyes as she slowly nodded an acknowledgement.

Still looking at the wall, LaRae murmured. "I used to hear of reports about women who were abused. And I wondered how they could stay with men who could hurt them. Then I found out for myself. It's all too easy. You believe the apologies and the promises. Then you look in the mirror and tell yourself the bruises will heal."

"Poor child."

"It wasn't so bad at first. His jealousy was kind of cute. It meant he cared. His demands and questions seemed almost indifferent. Then one day he lost his temper and slapped me. I don't even remember what it was about. He said he was sorry and it would never happen again. I thought it was because he was under stress from the business deal he was trying to work out."

Shirley silently pictured the harsh images that LaRae's soft monotone voice described as she waited for her to continue. What kind of a man would terrify the woman who had trusted him enough to marry him—to share her life with him? It was so hard for her to imagine such a man when her own Jacob had been so gentle and loving all his life.

LaRae's voice remained toneless as she continued. "Each time afterwards his hand-slaps became harder and harder until he was hitting with his fists and kicking with his feet. There were no more apologies—only angry words. I started to get scared then. I tried so hard not to make him mad. I tried to be a good wife. But I was always doing something wrong, always messing something up or saying the wrong thing."

"LaRae, no! It wasn't your fault. You were not to blame for what happened to you." Shirley tried to reassure her.

"Wasn't I? I stayed with him. Even after I knew it wasn't going to get any better. And I kept trying to be a good wife. I'd see the change in his face or attitude and instantly start apologizing even though I didn't know what I had done wrong. He would tell me it was my fault; that I made him do it, and I believed him. And one time when he had to take me to the doctor, I even lied and said what he told me to say. I know the doctor knew what happened, but James, as always, somehow convinced him not to report it."

Shirley gathered the woman in her strong arms and rocked her gently back and forth, tenderly reassuring her as she did. Immediately LaRae's guard came up and she pulled away quickly. The tears that LaRae fought so hard to hold back came flooding forth, as Shirley reached out to her.

"It's time to stop running. I'm going to put a call in to the sheriff." Shirley firmly stated after all LaRae's tears were spent.

"It won't do you any good. I've already told you James is a very powerful and wealthy man. He intimidates the authorities and the ones he can't intimidate he buys off. Either way, they all look the other way."

"Not this sheriff. He can't be bought.

"I told you they all can be bought. James has done it too many times. After He gets through with them, I'm the one they look upon as the perpetrator, the person that did something wrong." LaRae was frustrated with trying to explain herself. "If I don't leave and James finds me, just my being here will bring great danger to you and your guest. He's not a man to cross, because he is dangerous"

"I'm telling you the sheriff in this town is one that can't be intimidated or bought. He's my nephew and he is a strong Christian man." Shirley waited until she had LaRae's full attention before speaking once more, "Let me call him and I'll talk to him first for you."

LaRae didn't know what being a Christian had to do with anything, but she did know James Ashcroft and he always got his way. She shrugged as she spoke, "Go ahead but I'm telling you it won't do any good. I've been through this too many times."

LaRae went back to her packing ignoring the frustrated look on Shirley's face.

"At least hold off on your packing until I talk to Jason." Shirley said as she gently took the clothing from LaRae's hands and led her to a chair.

"Jason?" LaRae inquired.

"Jason Blanks, the sheriff. My nephew! He should be in his office about now. You wait here while I go call him." Shirley said as she went out the door closing it behind her.

LaRae, startled, jumped from the chair as a knock sounded upon her bedroom door. "I must have dozed off," she thought as she hurried to open the door.

"Jason is waiting at the gazebo in the garden to talk to you. I thought it would be more private out there for you two to talk, than in the house."

LaRae picked up her medium weight jacket off the top of the suitcase that still remained open on her bed, as she passed by it on her way out of the room.

After descending the stairs and walking through the dining room to the kitchen, LaRae stopped at the back door and turned in time to see Shirley in front of the stove. She removed the lid from one of the pots and began to stir the ingredients with a large wooden spoon. LaRae patiently waited for Shirley to finish. Shirley noticing LaRae had paused and was waiting for her to complete the task at hand waved LaRae on out the door.

"You go on ahead and I will join y'all when I finish here," She said as she turned her attention back to the pot she was stirring on the stove. LaRae reluctantly continued out the door, to the screened-in back porch, down the back steps and slowly walked toward the garden.

"Why are you doing this? She said to herself. Why are you putting yourself through this once again? You already know how this is going to turn out, so just turn around go upstairs and get your things and get out of here before it's too late."

LaRae was doing what come naturally, protecting herself the only way she knew how. Running.

Upon entering the garden, LaRae stopped, shaded her eyes, and studied with keen curiosity, the man that stood under the large oak tree near the gazebo a little ways from her. He wore a blue uniform that fit him perfectly. Made for him, she decided as her gaze traveled up his tall length to rest on a face, sculpted in strong clean lines. At this point, she recognized him as the police officer, which frequently visited the *Bed & Breakfast* each evening.

He turned and centered a set of observant blue eyes, that seemed to pierce straight through to her vary soul, immediately upon her movement. His curious regard trapped her momentarily wiping all reason from her mind.

"Ms. Carter or is it Ms. Jones?" He asked as he reached his hand out toward her.

LaRae shook the hand extended toward her and answered, "Its Jones, LaRae Jones." She allowed him to lead her toward a pair of chairs placed at an angle in the closed in gazebo.

Ordinarily being the sheriff, he wouldn't be the one handling an investigation of this type. He would hand it over to one of his deputies and send them out to look into the matter. But, as a favor to his Aunt Shirley he would be conducting the total investigation of the case. She believed in this woman and she was never wrong about people and he trusted her instinct.

Jason Blanks studied the petite women sitting across from him with keen interest. He could tell instantly she was withdrawn, frightened and in disguise. Although he must admit the contacts and wig did come closer to looking more authentic then anything else he had come across in a while

"Ms. Jones, my Aunt has already told me a lot about what is going on with you. I understand your ex-husband is stalking you. Is that correct?"

LaRae looked at him nervously and answered, "Yes."

"Can you give me his name and a physically description?"

"His name is James Allen Ashcroft. He is six foot two inches tall and weighs around two hundred and twenty five pounds." She paused before continuing, watching as the man before her wrote the information on a small notebook he held in his hand. Left-handed she noted to herself.

"And the color of his hair and eyes?" he asked seeing she was distracted. "He has brown eyes, jet-black curly hair, and a medium tanned complexion."

"Does he have any scars or tattoos?"

"Yes, he has a deep scare on the back of his right hand where he put it through a glass door in one of his fits of rage."

"Is there anything else you'd like to add that you think would be significant to the case?"

"I don't know if it's important but he's very meticulous with his dressing and grooming." Feeling stupid, as she usually did around men in authority, she added, "Maybe that's not important at all."

A couple of hours later, hearing the back screen door quietly open then close, Shirley removed two coffee cups from the cupboard and placed them on the cabinet beside the coffee pot. Shirley, nodding her head toward the coffee pot said, "Fresh coffee in the pot," as the couple entered the back door to the kitchen.

"No thank you," LaRae said without even a glance in Shirley's direction. Never breaking stride she made her way through the kitchen all the way to the entryway and up the stairs, making sure she politely smiled to all she met along the way. Once in her room, she quietly closed the door behind her before collapsing in a trembling heap on the bed.

Shirley patiently waited for her nephew to pour a cup of coffee, sweeten it to his taste and then take a seat at the small table across from her.

"Well?" She asked unable to restrain her curiosity any longer.

"Well, if she's telling the truth…"

"If she's telling the truth!" Shirley broke in with the harsh tone she had never used with her nephew before. She jumped up from the table and went to the stove and picked up her large wooden spoon and commenced to vigorously stir the ingredients in the large pot before her. She slowly turned around and faced her nephew, "let me tell you something Jason Blanks, if I know nothing else I know fear when I see it, and that young woman is afraid. She is afraid of her own shadow and someone or something put that fear in her. So don't sit there and say if she's telling the truth. How can you not believe her?" The whole time while she had been speaking, Shirley had been pointing and shaking her long wooden spoon at her nephew.

Jason had never seen his aunt so roused up. Slowly approaching her, he said, "Wait a minute I never said I didn't believe her."

Removing the spoon from her hand, he took his aunt in his arms and hugged her close. After Shirley calmed down some, Jason continued, "I never said I didn't believe Ms. Jones, but if what she says is true you and all guest could be in danger." Shirley slowly stepped back noting the seriousness on her nephew's face.

"What do you intend to do?"

"After seeing Ms. Jones for myself I have a plan."

"And that plan is…?"

"Officer Morgan will be living here in Ms. Jones room and Ms.

Jones will be moved into Officer Morgan's apartment where we will have her under twenty-four hour protection."

Shirley interrupted him, "Becky does have about the same build, and does have the same hair coloring as LaRae but that's where the similarities stop. They don't look anything alike in facial features."

"Exactly, Jason stated. Officers Morgan is to be herself. But her pretense will be that she has moved into the *Bed & Breakfast* because she works the night shift and all the noise of the renovations taking place at the apartment complex is depriving her of sleep."

Shirley nodded her head in agreement and taking her spoon back from Jason returned her attention to the food in the large pots simmering on her stove.

"Oh, Jason suddenly remembered, fix your guest registry to where it shows that last Sunday Nancy Carter checked out and Becky Morgan checked into her vacated room."

"I will." Shirley, then, gave her full attention to the pots on her stove. She had complete confidence that Jason would take care of everything, now that he was in control. "Everything would be all right," Shirley told herself.

Jason, glancing at the ceiling, asked. "Do you think she will be okay for the rest of the night?"

"You wait here and I'll go check on her."

Jason poured another cup of coffee and set back down at the table to wait.

"Don't let my stew burn or you'll be buying supper for everybody." Shirley laughed at the surprised look on his face as she left the room.

Returning to the kitchen, Shirley noted the serious look on her nephew's face. "What has you so deep in thought?"

"I think I'll stay here for the night. Do you have my old room rented out?" While his aunt was upstairs with her guest, Jason made some phone calls to make arrangements for protecting Ms. Jones. He didn't have the whole plan worked out completely, yet, but enough to set things into motion.

"What's going on, Jason?" Shirley could tell her nephew was worried. Even though he lived in a small two-bedroom house of his own on the same property, the only time he stayed at the *Bed & Breakfast* was during times of inclement weather or during special holidays.

"What makes you think anything's wrong? Maybe I just want to sleep in my old room and spend some time with my favorite aunt." He grinned from ear to ear.

"Jason Blanks you can run that blarney by somebody that doesn't know you as well as I do, and besides I'm the only aunt you have." She gave him a quick grin. "What's really going on?" Since the death of her husband, Jacob, Jason had taken on the role of her protector.

Jacob and she raised Jason from the age of nine after a drunk driver killed his parents, her sister Alice and her husband, Robert Blanks, in a head-on car crash. Looking at Jason, she reminded herself it had been over twenty-five years ago since the accident happened. They were out on a Friday night; Robert made reservation for a quite dinner to celebrate their fourteenth wedding anniversary. He asked me ahead of time if I would mind watching Jason for them while they go out for the night. Of course I didn't mind, they were hard-working, Christian people who never went any where without their son. The next thing we knew the hour was late and a policeman was knocking at our door. He informed us of the accident and that both of Jason's parents were killed on impact. "Thank God, he wasn't in the car with them or we would have lost all three of them." Shirley whispered to herself. Jason gave her a curious look.

Jason interrupted her thoughts. "I just want to be here incase this Ashcroft fellow comes around before I can get Ms. Jones out of here and situated into Officer Morgan's apartment complex."

"So you do believe her—and that the man is as dangerous as she said he was."

"I told you that I never said I didn't believe her."

Jason Blanks drove the short distance down the gravel road

between his small but cozy home, which was located on the back half of his aunt's property, and the *Bed & Breakfast*. Soon after showering and packing two days changing of clothing along with toiletries in a small bag he was driving back up the dirt road toward the *Bed & Breakfast* for the evening.

CHAPTER 6

Two weeks had passed since the exchange of the two women had taken place. Patrolman Betty Morgan, after settling into her room at Shirley's *Bed & Breakfast*, not only continued her regular night patrol duties, but also made sure to be seen around town frequently during the day as asked by the Sheriff. She never followed the same routine. Sometimes she would go to the local café for breakfast or linger over a couple of cups of coffee in the morning after she got off duty. Other times she would go to her room at Shirley's place and sleep for a while, then drop into the local café for a cup of coffee and then visit the local shops around the town square. She was discreetly making sure to be seen about town—hoping to be mistaken for LaRae. Constantly on the alert and always observant of someone following her, she made her designated rounds.

Because Sheriff Jason Blanks believed LaRae Jones' life to be in danger, he placed her in an apartment two apartments from Officer Morgan's two-bedroom apartment a the Sky Hawk apartment complex under the cover of darkness. This was apartment 1B. Calling in a couple of favors and borrowing six detectives from two other counties he now had her under twenty-four-hour protection. He knew these detectives personally and could vouch for their integrity and character. He could trust them with his own life. Their jobs beside protection were surveillance, observation of the complex, surrounding area, and the road into the complex for anything out of the ordinary—anything that did not belong.

He first moved in two of his own department's detectives, Ann Harris and Ray Kuntz, which he placed directly in the apartment with LaRae. Their orders where to come and go as any ordinary couple but never leave LaRae alone at any time. LaRae was never to be seen outside of the apartment.

A few days later he assigned detectives, Peggy Smith and Tyler Homes to the apartment on the left into apartment 1A. In apartment 1C to the right were detectives Jane Peel and John Smith. Their orders were about the same as Ann and Ray's; to come and go as an ordinary couple but for someone to always be in the apartment at all times.

And in apartment 2B upstairs directly over the apartment in which LaRae was hidden were detectives Don Turner and Frank Frye. These two detectives were picked for their sharpshooter skills and for their keen eye. A telescope had been set up in this apartment where detectives, Turner and Frye, could keep a continuous up-close watch on the apartment complex and beyond the surrounding area. They were never to leave the apartment except under the cover of darkness.

*

"How's it going?" Shirley asked as she poured her nephew a coup of coffee, and sat n the chair across from him.

"Nothing so far. Maybe he took the bait."

"Bait?" She asked with a questioning look upon her face.

"Yes, I had LaRae go by the hospital and drop a small hint in front of the right people that her next assignment would be taking her to Oregon before we placed her in a sanctuary."

"The look on your face is telling me a different story."

"I just don't know. Something just doesn't feel right about it."

"It?" Shirley asked puzzled by his statement.

"I want to believe the man bought the bait and is in Oregon. But my gut tells me he didn't and if he didn't then that means he's here. If he is I hope he makes a move soon because I only have them six borrowed detectives for another week."

*

In a car parked just off the narrow road in among trees and bushes below a small hill, the man tapped his fingers restlessly against the steering wheel as he watched the lights go off one by one throughout the apartment he knew LaRae was being kept in. When the last light went out, he tossed the smoked cigarette out the window, and turned his gaze back to the apartment just visible in the distance through the trees. He hadn't had a chance to explore around the place yet. But he learned one thing since he had been watching over the last two nights and that was she wasn't alone. He knew how to spot a cop even without their uniform on. She was surrounded by cops. He had to play it cool for a while and take his time.

He hated waiting. He'd been entertaining himself for a while, enjoying her fear, thriving on it, thrilled each time she bolted like a scared rabbit. He should have paid more attention and he would have gotten to her long before this, but she seemed to know just when to pack and run. It was like someone would give her a warning just before he was ready to make his move. It was maddening to him. But playtime was over. She would not escape this time he would make sure, for it was time to teach her a lesson—her final lesson. This was a matter of self-respect and righting the wrong done to him by an ungrateful wife. How dare her leave him like she did, sneaking away like a thief in the night. How dare her challenge him. Who does she think she is? She was his wife! He owned her! She was his!

*

"How is LaRae holding up today?" Shirley asked as she poured Jason a second cup of coffee and sat his breakfast down before him.

"Okay, I think."

"You think?" She asked with a questioning look upon her face.

"Yes, she's not one to show much emotion."

"The look on your face is telling me that something is bothering you."

"I had to let the detectives I borrowed go back."

"And?" Shirley questioned as she stepped to the stove to stir the stew meat n the large pot.

"I…just don't know. Something just doesn't feel right."

"You said that before," Shirley replied, giving him a puzzled look. As she waited for him to continue, she picked up a knife and commenced to chop the different vegetables she had placed on the chopping board earlier.

Jason sat with a faraway look in his eyes as he pondered over LaRae Jones's present dilemma. He knew she was as scared as an ally cat of her ex-husband. From the information his office received about James Ashcroft, she had a right to be. He is definitely a shady character. Recent newspaper articles from Boston revealed his company was in a lawsuit with a couple of ex-clients over fraud and embezzlement of funds. The lawsuit has been abruptly halted due to the disappearance of two key witnesses. These two witnesses are the ex-clients that mysteriously disappeared.

Jason finally replied, "I believe he is here and has been for a while. He has just been waiting to make his move."

Jason picked up his cup and took a couple of slow sips before placing it back in the saucer before him. Turning to face his aunt he spoke. "Aunt Shirley you need to be praying, because I honestly don't know how this one's going to turn out. I just have the feeling that if he is as determined as he seems to be, then someone may end up badly hurt."

Seeing how concerned he really was she reassured him. "I have been praying about this and will continue to do so until it is over."

*

Danger hadn't been on LaRae's mind and she hadn't been on guard. Believing James or his henchman was in Oregon somewhere, she was supposed to be moving back into Shirley's place tomorrow. But tonight, she and Ann Harris had just finished a light supper and were having a lively conversation.

LaRae found Ann to be an intelligent and kind woman with a sense of humor. She made these difficult times of waiting for James to make a move bearable. It was so easy to get caught up in her lightheartedness and silly jokes, which helped LaRae, soon forget all her fears and concerns of James. Ann, also, had a practical side. She had a serious boyfriend of three years, but before taking their relationship to the next step, she wanted to further her education and career in law enforcement.

Changing the conversation to a more serious tone, Ann looks at LaRae and asked, "What are your plans after all of this is over with?"

Jolted back to present reality by Ann's words, LaRae responded, quietly, "Will this ever be over with?"

"Of course it will! You have to have more faith in God than that."

LaRae shot a quick look at Ann and for an instant had a moment of déjà vu. She was reminded of Cindy, because that sounded exactly like something she would say.

"It's difficult to believe my life will ever be any different after all I have been through. I also have trouble believing in a god that would let me go through all that I have been through at the hands of someone who was supposed to have loved me."

"God doesn't cause people to do evil, He allows them to make choices," Ann replied as she reached out and gently took LaRae's hand. "Because your ex-husband chose to do evil to you, doesn't diminish the fact that God loves you and has always protected your life through it all."

LaRae listened in earnest to what Ann said. It did seem that a lot of times an invisible hand was protecting her. Like the time she was able to make her final escape from James. She made the decision to leave him the night before she left because of a brutal beating she had received at his hands. She packed as much as she could in suitcases the next day and thought she was leaving before he got home. On her way out of the long narrow road to the highway she met James coming home from work. She expected him to see her and immediately block her path with his own car. The opposite happened! He drove on past! In fear, she constantly watched her rearview mirror for him to turn around and come after her, but it never happened. Actually, as he passed by her, he gave no indication that he ever saw her. There is no way he could not see her, it must have been the evening light and the setting sun. Even though LaRae knew James was traveling North on the narrow road as she was traveling south. All of this is too far fetched for her to believe even though she still ponders over the incident, often. She knew James and how obsessed he is with her.

LaRae not wanting to dwell on the religious factor anymore changed the subject. "I'm going to take my shower and turn in early. I'm really tired since I didn't sleep much last night."

"Okay…and I'll get mine later," Ann responded, walking to the window and peaking through the curtains surveying the parking lot and the area beyond.

While LaRae was taking her shower, Ann checked to make sure all doors and windows were securely locked. When LaRae emerged from the bathroom, the two women said goodnight to one another and Ann proceeded to the bathroom to take her own shower. After her shower and before retiring for bed, Ann turned all light off and checked to see that LaRae was safely in bed.

LaRae, restless and unable to sleep wandered out into the apartment complex's enclosed courtyard. How could she of been so foolish, she would later reflect.

"LaRae."

The voice LaRae heard every night in her nightmares suddenly was there in the shadows. It might have been just a whisper on the wind but it was there, calling her name. The fear she had lived with for so long was realized at that very moment. It consumed her, freezing her in time and space. She wanted to run, turn and hide but she couldn't move. LaRae forced herself to turn around slowly searching the dark shadows from where the voice was originating.

"Darling, aren't you glad to see your husband?" James spoke in a sharp contemptible low voice.

She kept waiting for him to emerge.

"You look so surprised, Darling." He said in the calm tone that had always preceded violence.

"Weren't you expecting me?"

His cruel laugh sent tremors throughout her body destroying her desire, her self-confidence, reducing her to a cornered animal.

LaRae swallowed hard several times but her voice still wouldn't come. After several more tries, in a trembling voice she cried, "Why can't you just leave me alone?"

The reflection of the moonlight off the gun in his hand was the first thing to catch LaRae's attentions as James slowly walked from the shadows before her. Fear causing her to put more distance between them left her unaware of the fact she was also putting distance between her and the safety of the apartment.

"You shouldn't have left me. I told you I keep what belongs to me."

"We're divorced." She whispered.

"You're my wife and always will be. You belong to me. I have the papers to prove it." He laughed harshly.

Wrapping her arms tightly about her own waist, LaRae pleaded, "Stop, please don't do this."

James didn't seem to hear her. "I made you mine. Remember your vows, till death do we part. A court can't put the marriage asunder. You will only be free of me in death."

LaRae cringed from his words. Her whole body trembled uncontrollably. Every cell in her body was consumed with fear, and she knew she was in an enclosed courtyard with a deadly enemy. Now she knows how the fox feels on a foxhunt, except the fox gets a head start in an open area.

James pointed the gun toward her.

"Move."

She was motionless. She couldn't move, if she wanted to. It seemed to her that an eternity had passed, but only minutes had gone by since she had first heard her name whispered upon the wind.

"I said move!" Came his menacing voice.

This time he pointed toward the far end of the courtyard with the gun to put emphasis on his words.

"You know I've just been biding my time. It was kind of fun watching you run like a scared rabbit. I knew sooner or later it was just a matter of time before you'd get caught in my trap, little rabbit." He laughed sarcastically with the last words.

Slowly LaRae turned and advanced through the turns and twists of the courtyard garden in the direction in which James had pointed her toward. After advancing a short distance to an open setting area, he directed her toward the shadows. From this point on he made sure their movements were kept hidden in the shadows. Knowing that each step carried her further from safety, LaRae stayed on constant alert for some way to escape.

With James being so close to her it brought back all the memories. The cruel intrusions reminding her of the scars James had left her with. LaRae closed her eyes tightly as she tried to push the memories away. She stumbled along in the darkness, trying to push away the past hurts from her mind.

LaRae lurched forward her arms instantly stretched out into the darkness grasping at the air for something to break her fall. She collided hard with the ground hitting her knee on something sharp. She winced at the pain as she tried to get up.

James roughly jerked her from the ground and set her on her feet. A slight cry of pain escaped from her tight lips when she put weight on the leg with the injured knee. He forcefully pushed her forward.

"Keep moving," came his low growled words.

The closer they moved toward the opposite end of the courtyard, LaRae noticed the moonlight reflecting off something shiny behind the bushes across the road. The knowledge of what that something was hit her immediately. In her reeling mind was a single sickening realization of what would happen if she allowed him to maneuver her into that automobile and drive away. She would not allow herself to be carried away from here in it. If James was going to kill her he would have to do it here, because she was not taking another step and LaRae stopped walking abruptly.

"Keep moving." James hissed at her.

"No!"

"I'll blow you away, and nobody will ever know it was me. I've got witnesses to say I'm at home in a meeting right now."

"You probably do, you always did have everything covered."

"Don't push your luck."

She heard herself speak as if from a great distance, the threat of death no longer a threat.

"Let me tell you something, you have forced me to run, to hide, and to look over my shoulder in terror for years. You have almost destroyed me on several occasions. You have shattered my self-respect, humiliated and degraded me; you have beaten me and hurt me to the point of turning me into a cowering caged animal."

LaRae took a slow deep breath and pulled herself up to all her five feet in height. She wasn't even looking at the gun he held in his hand she was staring him straight in his face when she next spoke.

"If you're going to kill me you're to do it here and now, because I'm not going any further with you, and you can believe I'm not getting into any automobile with you."

Her unexpected defiance momentarily stunned James just enough that LaRae was able to knock him off his feet by throwing her whole body weight into him. She continued on past him and kept going as fast as her injured leg would allow her to run. Even though the pain in her knee hampered her escape, she knew she could not stop; she had to make it back to the apartment and safety.

LaRae took the shortest route back to the apartment, which was through the center of the courtyard. This path was wider and well lit at night. James had to be drawn from the shadows in order for eyewitnesses to be able to place him here in Arkansas. This was her only hope.

Hearing a loud thud, LaRae slowed her stride and turned just in time to see a collision between Jason and James; the force of the impact carried both men to the ground. She saw both men go down. The hard crash knocked them apart so they could roll and move quickly to their feet. Jason was first up, forceful and quick, but James, furious, was almost as fast.

It happened so fast that LaRae couldn't move a muscle. Then remembering the gun, she looked around wildly for it. The realization hit her immediately when she could not locate it that it had to of been knocked to the ground among the flowerbeds about the courtyard or the shrubs lining the pathway.

It seemed to her that an eternity had passed, but only minutes had gone by. She kept her eyes fixed on the two men. James couldn't stand losing. With the survival instinct of an animal, he took advantage of every opportunity. The sickening thuds of flesh made LaRae cringe. The marks of battle were showing on both men. James had a split lip and one eyed looked swollen from where Jason's large first made several quick jackhammer direct hits. LaRae noted a reddening mark high on Jason's left cheekbone that would eventually become a bruise. Jason hastily swiped at the blood that dripped from his mouth before throwing several rapid hard blows to James' midsection and head that knocked him to the ground.

James rolled twice on the ground before coming to his knees and brandishing the gun he used to threaten LaRae with earlier. James had no comprehension of fair play and she knew he'd pull something deceitful if he got the chance.

"Jason, gun!" LaRae shouted seeing the moonlight's reflection instantly.

"Drop the gun, Ashcroft. It's over." Jason commanded.

"What?" He barked, obviously having no idea how ridiculous the demand sounded since he held the gun.

James's eyes fixed on LaRae. His voice was cold and harsh when he spoke, "You shouldn't have left me. I told you I keep what is mine."

"You will never get out of here. The whole area is surrounded." Jason told him.

LaRae tried her best not to allow him to see her fear. She gathered all her inner strength and never showing fear looked James straight in the face, yet never spoke a word. James stared at the scared rabbit he had hurt and trailed for years, and he saw in her stony gaze something that frightened him. She was no longer terrified. She had conquered him simply by overcoming her fear of him.

With a thunderous blind rage he pointed the gun at her and cocked the hammer. Two swift shots splintered the air, almost deafening and so powerful they sounded like one. A look of shock covered his face as James pitched backwards and fell heavily to the ground. A crimson think liquid seeped onto his shirt from the holes in the area over the center of his chest.

Ann Harris emerged from among the shadows immediately with her gun in a steady two-handed grip aimed at James lying on the ground. She approached Jason where they spoke softly for a few minutes before she turned and headed in LaRae's direction. Frozen stiff and in stunned silence, Ann wrapped her arm around LaRae's shoulder and gently turned her from the scene in front of her.

"Come on let me get you back to the apartment so Jason can call in the paramedics."

Trembling uncontrollably and limping, LaRae allowed Ann to lead her toward the apartment without saying a word. Once inside Ann led LaRae to the sofa and gently pushed her down. Then, retrieving extra pillows from the bedrooms brought them back to the living room and placed them under LaRae's leg with the injured knee. Then, she made some ice packs and placed them around the injured area.

"Ouch!" LaRae cringed in pain.

"The paramedics will take a look at you when they conclude outside." After answering questions Jason could not respond to for her, the paramedics were soon at her side examining her knee and decided to load her up in the ambulance and take her to the emergency room, the ER doctor determined she must be admitted. An orthopedic surgeon would be called in to look at her knee and x-rays tomorrow.

Sleep that night came hard for LaRae and when it finally did come, it was restless—full of twisted nightmarish images of the night's event over and over. She sees James with the gun in hand as he turns and aims it toward her, and hears the two quick shots. Yet, she sees the bullets leave the barrel of the pistol and feels the pain as they hit their target dead center of her chest—not his. The thick crimson liquid flowed covering the white blouse she was wearing. It continues to flow until it was running off her onto the ground she lay upon. This crimson liquid continued to stretch out before her like lava from an active volcano until everything was covered with it.

LaRae awoke trembling in fear and covered in sweat, not remembering exactly where she was. It all gradually came back to her as she thought on the events that took place the evening before. After collecting her wits about her, she rang for the nurse and asked for help in changing her nightgown. Because her knee was hurting her, painfully, she also asked for some pain medication. But sleep evaded her and soon it was morning and a nurse was bringing her a breakfast tray and informing her that the doctor would be in soon to make an assessment of her injured knee.

LaRae was ready for some answers for herself, which could only be obtained by talking to Jason and Ann. As she was thinking on this, she heard a knock on the door and speaking loudly, she called, "Come in."

The door opened and in walked Jason. LaRae greeted him with a big smile as a sensation of deep gratitude and a feeling of calm swept over her at his appearance. Someone else was trailing behind him, but LaRae paid no attention to that person, at first, thinking it was most likely hospital personnel. Her thoughts were consumed with questions for Jason concerning James. Soon she looked and noticed the man behind Jason and suddenly terror gripped her. She immediately threw the covers off of her and swung her legs over the side of the bed in an attempt to run. She yelled to Jason, "Run" as she tried to bear weight on her injured leg, but fell to the floor in the attempt to do so.

"LaRae, LaRae, calm down! What's wrong?" Jason demanded, rushing to her.

"That's...that's...that's the man that's been following me!" LaRae cried, stumbling over her words.

Jason could see the fear in her eyes. He picked her up and placed her back on the bed—all the time telling her everything is all right. "He's one of the good guys. He's been helping us."

"I don't understand. Why was he following me, then?" She asked peeking around Jason's broad shoulder to have another look at the man.

"LaRae, I want you to meet Gilbert Garth," Jason said as he moved aside so they each could see one another. "Gilbert, this is LaRae Jones, the young lady whose ex-husband hired you to find and follow.

"Hi Ms. Jones," he greeted with a smile. "You were a hard one to keep up with."

LaRae looking him straight in the face asks, "It was you at the masquerade ball, right?"

He smiled mischievously and answered, "Yes ma'am, it was. Sorry I frightened you. You're quite a tiger when you're angered."

"And the white sedan?"

"Yes ma'am, that was me too."

"What about the telephone calls?"

"A few of those were mine, but I am sure not all were. I tried to be as unobtrusive as possible over the phone, but that didn't work. You were always too alert," he said with a big smile spread across his face.

LaRae gave Gilbert Garth a dismissive look and turned her attention to Jason. She had so many unanswered questions.

"How did you know James was going to be there last night?" She asked.

"I wasn't positive, but I knew he was in the area."

"How?"

"Gilbert Garth, here, showed up in my office with a story to tell."

"So that's how he would always find me so quickly. What did you have to say?" she asked, turning her attention back to Gilbert.

"I wanted to know for myself what was really going on since too many things didn't add up and I had seen on several occasions Mr. Ashcroft's temper flair. So, I did some checking into your ex-husband's background after the assignment he hired me to do for him."

"And"

"After talking to your attorney that handled your divorce, I also talked to the doctor at the hospital that treated you when you were so badly beaten and were taken in for treatment."

LaRae cringed at the remembrance of all she had suffered at the hands of James. Jason noticing the expression of pain on her face gently took her hand and picked up the conversation.

"Mr. Garth has been following Ashcroft every since the conclusion of his employment with him. He knew that a man like Ashcroft would never bring a weapon registered in his own name across stateliness, and even though gun laws are strict a man like Ashcroft who is use to getting what he wants, would find a way around this. So Mr. Garth followed him to a small pawn shop in the area, where he observed Ashcroft purchasing the weapon that he used last night."

"So after talking to Mr. Garth you knew for sure he was in the area?"

"Yes, and that he was frequently in the area around the

apartments. One of my men spotted a strange car parked some distance from the highway not far from the apartments a couple of days ago. My office checked it out and found out it was a rental car. So we kept a watch on it and soon discovered it was Ashcroft. We had to wait till he made a move before we could do anything."

LaRae inhaled sharply then exhaled slowly before asking, "Mr. Garth did you tell James I was her? Is that how he found me?"

"No, I haven't worked for him in a while. I have been trying to find out what Ashcroft was up to."

"Now what?" LaRae asked her voice just above a whisper.

"There will be a coroner's hearing," Jason replied, "there won't be much to it."

"Then James is...dead?"

"Yes." Jason answered as gentle as he could.

LaRae lapsed into stony silence and when she spoke again she said, "I would like to be alone now, please."

Jason and Gilbert were startled at how quick she withdrew into herself. But neither questioned her and quickly bid her goodbye, reassuring her she had nothing to worry about now. All of her fears of James Ashcroft are over with and he can never hurt her again.

After closing the door behind them upon leaving, LaRae gazed out the hospital window as a flood of thoughts, never before thought of, pierced her mind. *"Free! Free at last. Free from the grips of the horror that I lived with for so, so many years. James is dead? How could that be? He can't be dead! He had to be alive to pursue me! No...He is dead!"* LaRae kept going back and forth with this scenario in her mind. It was almost too real to be true and even harder to comprehend. Finally, she settled on the realization of the fact that James is indeed dead. *"I saw and heard the gunshots and the bullets as they entered his chest. I saw him fall to the ground. I saw the blood flow from his body. Dead...James is dead!"*

CHAPTER 7

After a rather lengthy stay in the hospital from knee replacement surgery, LaRae, in her condition, would need help until she could get back on her feet again. Not having family of her own in the area, she had been discharged into Shirley's caring hands.

"Be careful boys and bring her straight back this way." Shirley directed the two men, who were helping LaRae out of the car and into the house; while at the same time she kept a close eye on LaRae for any signs of pain.

"I have a room all set up for her down the hall."

Once Shirley helped LaRae change her clothing and get into bed, she arranged pillows around the bed to try and make her friend as comfortable as possible.

"I've placed your walker here in easy reach by the nightstand...incase you have to get up during the night...this room has a bathroom attached so you don't have to go down the hall."

"I just don't know how to thank you for what you're doing for me."

"Just getting better is enough thanks for me."

"Well, I'm going to say it anyway." LaRae paused just for a second. "Thank you...my friend!" LaRae reached out and took Shirley's hand to add emphasis to her words.

LaRae actually considered Shirley a true, trustworthy friend. Every since the night before she was put in hiding, she was able to open up and talk to Shirley about the pain deep inside of her. This woman standing before her did not judge her or put her down as a bad person.

This woman just offered comforting arms and soothing words.

"Thank you Baby Doll, for being my friend." With those words Shirley gave LaRae's hand a gentle squeeze then leaned over and kissed her forehead. Shirley has been calling LaRae, her Baby Doll, every since the night she found out who she really was and the terrible truth about her ex-husband.

"Now try and get some rest. I've placed your pain medication here by this glass and a fresh pitcher of water on the nightstand." Shirley turned to leave the room. "Do you need anything else before I go?"

"No I don't think so."

Shirley opened the door and turned off the light in the room before leaving. Immediately LaRae was overcome with a strong sense of fear.

"Oh, please leave the light on." LaRae feeling like she sounded childish added, "incase I have to get up in the night…I don't want to trip over something."

Shirley hearing the panic in the young woman's voice, even though she tried hard to hide it, turned the room's overhead light on. She then walked around the bed and turned on a small lamp displayed on a table beside a chair in the corner of the room.

"How's that? Do you think that will be enough light during the night?" Shirley asked kindly before walking back around the bed.

"That'll be perfect. Thank you." LaRae responded softly.

LaRae was ashamed of the fact she could not sleep without at least a dim light on. James had made her this way. All her running and hiding, the anxiety over the unknown, along with her constant visuals, she had grown use to dim lights in close proximity to her at all times. She knew it made no sense because James was dead and buried. Yet, the fear of him still remained.

It had been two days since her discharge from the hospital. The physical therapist would be arriving today to instruct her on the exercises that would be needed to strengthen her knee. Awakening early and wanting to tend to her personal hygiene, LaRae gathered her change of clothing and placed it in the case hanging from the front of her walker; she then slowly walked across the room and opened the bathroom door.

Upon finishing in the bathroom she opened the door to walk the short distance back to the bed to await the arrival of the physical therapist. Suddenly, a hazy mist almost obscured her vision, and the sound of her own breathing was loud in her ears. Her mouth began to water causing her to constantly swallow. Sweat beaded across her forehead and also ran down the back of her neck. Leaning heavily upon the metal walker, and dragging herself over to the bedside, she lowered her body down on the edge of the bed. Panting, she slumped back against the headboard, trying to gather her strength; she had to maneuver her legs upon the bed, and she had only a few moments left before passing out.

The dreams were still so hazy that it was several minutes before she realized she was awake, but awareness did not necessarily bring insight. She lay quietly, looking around the cool, dim, room and groping for any details in her mind that would give her a hint of what was going on and where she was. Then she heard the well-known voice.

"Are you feeling better now, Baby Doll?" Shirley asked, lightly wiping LaRae's forehead with a damp cloth.

"Yes, thank you...I don't know what happened." LaRae responded faintly.

She moved cautiously, her mouth clinched at the amount of effort it took. There was throbbing pain in her left knee and she had a dull headache above her eyes. Awkwardly, she threw back the coverlet and struggled to straighten her position. Dizziness, once again, overcome her, but she gripped the side of the bed until the feeling subsided, and then she looked at Shirley and smiled.

"You shouldn't have been out of bed by yourself...you're still too weak." Shirley chastened her gently.

LaRae wanted to argue with her friend but knew there was no sense in it. That was the truth, LaRae thought depressingly. She was exhausted, as if she'd run a marathon; her legs felt as if they were made of rubber. Her exhaustion was changing into acute sleepiness. As if on cue, Shirley touched her face, with fingers cool and light. "Go to sleep," she said. "I'll wake you when the physical therapist gets here."

Quietly Shirley left the room and went to the kitchen, where she found Jason with cup in hand approaching the table to sit down in his favorite place.

"How's she doing today?" he asked when he saw his aunt enter the room.

"Trying to do too much too soon…that's a stubborn one she is." Shirley firmly replied.

"Sounds like someone else I know" Jason tried to hide his chuckle but was unsuccessful. "Maybe that's why y'all get along so well."

Her movements smooth, she set beef tips simmering for beef stew and began dicing potatoes, carrots, and celery. This meal would not be ready by the time LaRae finished with physical therapy; her lunch would consist of a bowl of soup, a sandwich and a glass of milk. The beef stew would be served with homemade bread and fresh vegetables to her guest for supper.

Shirley looked up from where she was preparing the food at the work island to look directly at Jason.

"I found her past out—white as a ghost—half dangling off the bed."

"Is she okay?" Shirley could hear the concern he tried to hide in his voice.

"Now she is." She replied, after pouring a cup of coffee and joining her nephew at the table. "I helped her get settled back into bed, she's resting now; but only after I promised to wake her when the physical therapist arrived."

The two were content to set quietly for awhile enjoying each others company, before Shirley spoke, "she's pushing herself too hard, it hasn't been quite three weeks since she had her surgery." Shirley pushed her body out of the chair and walked to the work island, where she picked up the cutting board and scraped the diced vegetables from it into the pot with the beef tips; then turned the knob on the front of the stove to lower the fire under the pot.

*

It was winter and a new layer of snow had fallen in the night, not more than an inch or two on top of what already lay on the ground. Just enough new snow, to soften the edges along the path Jason had shoveled from the house to the garage and, knowing how much LaRae loved to walk the pathway; he also cleared all the way to the gazebo. The sky was so blue it almost hurt to look at it. The new fallen snow is so pure-white and perfect, LaRae thought, as she with cane in hand continued to carefully pick her way down the pathway.

LaRae loved the wintertime with the new fallen snow glistening like diamonds in the sun. All seemed wonderful till she remembered at one time how she had congratulated herself on marrying into a wonderful family with such handsome, charming men. But, that was when she'd believed in the elegant performances James put on, and well before she'd learned that the only thing real about him were the lies that slipped from his lips so easily. After moving her away from her family, James had been as sparing with money as he had been with affection; and far too free with disapproval and his fist. With a long sigh she continued down the path.

Approaching the front of the gazebo, she entered in and made herself comfortable. A bitter anguish fresh in her mind as her thoughts continued in the past. She's not the same girl she used to be, with romantic dreams. "No, because of James, that part of her was gone forever" she said softly. Her words lost on the quiet wafts of wind blowing around the gazebo. "And what of it?" She asked herself fiercely. What good came from mourning what couldn't be changed? If she lost her old dreams, she'd have to find new ones to replace them with, if it were even possible.

LaRae thought of life as a dramatic novel, a great author had penned. The plot had been written. She was only one of the many characters; she really had no "say so" as to how it would be performed. Alas, it was too late now; one couldn't go back now and change it. The book had been bound and published. The parts were cast. The play would go on as composed. LaRae could only play her role out to the end.

LaRae's thoughts were abruptly interrupted when she heard someone call her name.

"Aunt Shirley wants to know if you're about ready for lunch." Jason asked finding her deep in thought in the gazebo. LaRae appreciated Jason escorting her back over the path to the house, where she thanked him and took her leave to go to her room and freshen up for lunch.

She paused before entering the dining room; this would be the first time in a long time that she would be taking her meal with the small group. She noted that Shirley's only other two guest were already seated at the table, in deep conversation with Jason. Mr. Elton Potts, a gentleman in his early sixties had taken up residence at the *Bed & Breakfast* after his wife died, two and a half years earlier. He was a thoughtful man, who constantly had a kind word for everyone, had a receding hairline and, as he called it, a healthy waistline. The other guest was Max Cove, a college professor, in his fifties, of slender built and average height, never married, according to him, a nice man but stayed to himself a great deal busily grading student papers.

Jason must have said something funny that made Max laugh, the sound almost rusty, as if the man hadn't laughed in awhile. Tears of laughter gathered in the corner of the man's eyes; he pulled his handkerchief from his pocket and dabbed at the droplets. Soon all three men, no longer able to hold back their merriment, were cackling out loud.

Jason noticing LaRae entering the room stood up and walked to her chair to pull it out from the table for her to set down. She sat down lightly; the movement brought with it a whiff of some light, flowery scent. For just a moment he thought he was in a meadow of wild flowers instead of in the dining room of his aunt's home. The conversation flowed smoothly among the small group, once Shirley joined her guest, and as always the meal was excellent.

The group moved to the parlor for coffee and light conversation, where LaRae assumed her usual seat beside the fireplace. She tried hard to keep her mind on the discussion around her; in spite of that her thoughts drifted back into the past.

Before a church full of witnesses she had vowed to honor James, to cherish, and obey him. Though she had tried her hardest those first few months, she hadn't been able to be the wife he wanted her to be. As time past the harder she tried the worse the situation grew for her. The charming, kind man she thought she had married turned into a selfish and brutal beast of a man with a heart of stone.

"Baby Doll what do you think?" Shirley asked. "Jason wants us all to go Christmas tree hunting with him this year." She quickly added seeing LaRae was lost in thought.

Bleakly, LaRae fanned a smile, her head tipped to one side so the firelight turned her cheeks a flushed golden color and her blue eyes gleamed like sapphires from the moist tears reflected in the light. Swiftly, LaRae turned away back toward the hearth before anyone could see the tears in her eyes.

"What about the snow and ice?" LaRae asked tapping her cane for affect.

"She's got you there." Shirley laughingly said to Jason.

"I think the best idea is for you men to get the tree while LaRae and I get the decorations together."

"Sounds like a plan to me." Mr. Potts agreed not wanting the women traipsing around in the woods in this weather.

"Then it's agreed, next weekend we men will go find you the best Christmas tree you have ever had Aunt Shirley." Jason turned and looked at both men. "Right men!"

"Right." Mr. Potts and Professor Cove chimed in simultaneously.

Too soon the evening had turned to night, LaRae thought, the meal was completed, coffee in the parlor with light conversation had drawn to an end, and now all were bidding their "good nights" and off to their assigned rooms to sleep. LaRae detested this part of the twenty-four hour day, the night hours when most lay in peaceful slumber; she fought demons in nightmares of pure horror.

LaRae awoke with a shock. Confused, quivering and drenched in sweat; some unknown fear had her in its grasp again. Her heart was pounding, as she slowly looked around the room too terrified to move. She forced herself to take slow deep breaths as she looked at the clock on her bedside table. The sun would be rising in an hour or so, she thought, and banish the dark and the demons hiding in the shadows for another day. So why, then, was her heart still pounding, her breathing still erratic as if she'd run a hundred yard dash? By sheer will she fought back the nightmares of the past and focused instead on reality. She searched the room for something to focus on; her eyes fell upon the fire flickering in the fireplace. She despised the night hours.

Still struggling to control her emotions, the nightmare still fresh in her mind and the remembrance of the long ago bruised and swollen eyes; yet, she still didn't want it to end that way. Not like that, not with James dead. She just wanted him to leave her alone and let her have a life separate from him. Why can't you just leave me alone? Still you try to control me from the grave.

She crawled out of bed, removed the screen from in front of the fireplace and placed another log on the fire. Knowing there would be no more sleep for her, LaRae pulled the rocker closer to the fire, grabbed a quilt from the bed; and made herself comfortable waiting for the sun to rise. Gazing into the fire, she rocked slowly back and forth, listening for sounds of movement in the house, which would announce Shirley was up and ready to begin her day.

Once the snow stopped, it took Jason and Professor Cove two days to shovel the sidewalks in front of the house, as well as the paths that ran between the house and the garage and storage sheds. *Aunt Shirley's bursitis was right; it was going to be a long hard winter,* Jason thought dropping another shovelful of snow and then straightening himself. Breathing hard, he leaned on the shovel's handle to rest for a bit. To the right of him a little flock of birds scurried excitedly as they pecked about in the old vegetable garden for last year's leftovers that poked through the snow-covered ground. Smiling at their little bouncy motions, Jason lifted his hat to wipe the sweat from his forehead. The sky overhead was a brilliant blue, the newest snow sparkling like diamonds in a sun warm enough to drip long, glistening icicles from the eaves of the buildings.

Saturday morning dawned with a clear sunny blue sky, but bitter cold with a remainder of at least two inches of snow still on the ground. The three men donned their heavy coats, scarves, hats and gloves, and bid the women *good bye.* Shirley handed Jason a thermos full of hot coffee and a lunch box packed full of sandwiches.

"You men be careful, I don't want any of y'all coming back with any broken bones to be mended." Shirley said jokingly trying to hide her concern.

"We will Aunt Shirley." Jason kissed his aunt reassuringly on her cheek.

The women throwing on coats walked with the men out to the truck and watched as they climb into it, backed the old truck down the driveway, and then drove out of sight. After entering the house, the women removed their coats and hung them on hooks beside the back door. Shirley automatically started clearing the breakfast dishes from the table while LaRae ran warm water in the sink.

"I've got this, Baby Doll if you have something else to do." Shirley said while stacking the dishes on the cabinet closest to the sink.

"No, that's okay; I've got it, if you want to go start clearing a place for the men to put the tree when they get back."

"Okay, I'll be in the parlor," with those words Shirley turned and headed out of the kitchen.

"I'll join you when I finish here." LaRae agreed.

Supper was warming on the stove in the kitchen; the different Christmas decorations had been gathered sorted through and placed in the parlor where also a warm fire burned in the fireplace. The only thing missing were the men. The sun was about to set and the men had been gone all day; LaRae noted, if they didn't return soon Shirley would wear a whole in the antique rug, which covered the floor in the parlor, from her constant pacing back and forth to look out the window.

"They're here; we can set the table now!" Shirley exclaimed. LaRae followed her into the kitchen to help take up the food and place it on the table in the dining room. Just as the last bowl of hot food was situated on the table the men entered the back door. After stomping their boots free of snow and removing their outer garments they entered the dining room with joyful greetings.

"It took all day but we found you the perfect Christmas tree, Aunt Shirley." Jason said, stopping to kiss her on the cheek, before rounding the table to take his seat.

"Mmm something smells wonderfully good." Mr. Potts exclaimed as he took his place at the table.

"Truly was a wonderful adventure and I do agree with Jason you're going to like the specimen of tree we brought home for you." Professor Cove stated as he seated himself at his usual place around the table. The supper conversation consisted of the funny antics the men had during the day trying to find the "perfect" tree. First they had to find it, then once they found it how were they going to get to it; and last how were they going to bring it back home. The telling of the story had the women laughing excitedly.

With the meal over, the group withdrew to the parlor for coffee as they did every evening. The men had retrieved the tree from the truck and positioned it in the space Shirley had cleared, in front of the double windows. Each person took turns placing ornaments in different locations on the tree until the only one left was the angel for the top.

Shirley very carefully unwrapped it, and then gentle handed it to Jason to place on top. Using a small ladder and Shirley directing from below the angel took her rightful place on the tree.

"This is the second perfect Christmas tree I've ever had." Shirley said tearfully, wrapping her arms around her nephew's waist.

"The second?" Jason questioned. Jason knew the story but he also knew his aunt needed to visit that time in her past tonight.

"Yes, the second, the first perfect Christmas tree was your Uncle Jacob's and my very first Christmas. Like you men, he had spent all day, looking for the perfect tree to bring home to his new wife. He was so very proud when he brought that tree through the door. It was so full and tall, almost touching the ceiling without a stand. Not having much money in those days, he worked late at night, after work, carving and painting lovely ornaments to fill the tree. On Christmas Eve he surprised me with the magnificent angel that is placed on top of every tree to this day." Shirley dabbed at the tears gathering in the corners of her eyes.

"He was a fine man and a good uncle to me." Jason proclaimed then hugged his Aunt close. Then to change the somber mood of the room, jokingly asked, "are you sure this tree isn't the most perfect tree you ever had?" and danced her playfully around the room to the carols playing in the background. The whole group laughed at his frolicking.

The hour was late and all bid their nightly departures. Once again LaRae entered her room with trepidation; knowing she was alone to face the demons in the night. Changing into her nightgown, she pulled the rocker close to the fireplace and wrapped the quilt, which lay across the foot of the bed around her; then took what had become her nightly position in front of the hearth. Taking crochet hook and thread in hand, she started in on her project. Not being able to sleep at night she decided to fill those hours of darkness with making Christmas stockings for her friends, later she would fill each with candy canes and different types of candies.

No matter what LaRae tried she could not shut out James' voice.

It was always there in her head with its vile intimidating threats, accusations, and cutting remark. No longer did she sleep at night because he invaded her sleep in the form of nightmares; now he plagued her wakefulness with his constant assaults on her mind.

"I'm worried about her." Shirley said looking across the table at Jason.

"I admit she's not looking good." He took a sip of coffee before continuing. "She's looking awfully thin and has some bad dark circles under her eyes. Do you know what's going on with her?"

"No, but I know she's up late at night—she has that old fear back in her like before—she needs our prayers to help her get through what ever she's going through."

It was two days before Christmas Eve and LaRae still had not bought the first Christmas gift; so dressing warmly for the day, she let herself out the back door and cautiously made her way along the path to the garage. She slowly backed her SUV down the driveway and headed toward town. Once in town she parked her vehicle in a local parking area to all the shops, and then stepped out to move among the other late shoppers in and out of the different shops.

The first shop she entered was the tobacco shop where she purchased Professor Cove some of his favorite blend of pipe tobacco for his evening smoke on the back porch before retiring for the night. The second shop was a men's clothing shop where she purchased a tan sweater with brown leather patches on the elbows for Mr. Potts; she had noticed the blue one he was wearing now was missing a few buttons and the elbow patches were coming loose. LaRae continued searching through the store for the next person on her list, Jason, who turned out to be harder than she thought to buy for.

She ended up going to a unique gift shop a few shops down from the men's clothing store where she purchased a brass and pewter chess set stylistic of the Renaissance period with molded pieces shaped as kings, queens, knights, and even dragons. The last person on her list was Shirley and she knew just what she wanted to buy for her. LaRae crossed the road and headed for the antique shop on the corner. Upon entering the store she proceeded straight to the back corner where she had seen the dark blue velvet Victorian vanity set complete with two atomizers. She was starting to worry because she could not find it, then there it was pushed back to the side. Picking the set up and after inspecting it closely, she headed to the front of the store to check out.

After purchasing Shirley's favorite cologne, *Lilly of the Fields*, LaRae had one last stop to make, *The Old-style Candy Shop*, where she would purchase the candy canes and other Christmas candies for the crochet stockings she had made for her friends.

With her shopping done, LaRae returned to her room at Shirley's *Bed & Breakfast*; where she completed the task of wrapping the gifts purchased for her friends. With the task accomplished she placed the bags holding the different candies behind the drapes close to the window to help keep them cool until Christmas Eve. She didn't want any of the delicious chocolate treats to melt and she couldn't put them in Shirley's kitchen refrigerator where they would surely be found.

"Now if I can just get through this holiday and stay busy; that's the only way to block out his voice—that's the only way I'm going to be able to do it," she whispered to herself. LaRae had started speaking her thoughts quietly to herself when she was alone; it helped to hinder James' voice from getting through with it vile innuendos. She slipped out of her room and went directly to the kitchen where she found Shirley preparing the evening meal; she immediately grabbed an apron from the drawer and set in to help.

LaRae looked at Shirley curiously before speaking, "this close to Christmas and no pies, cookies, or cakes yet."

"I'm sorry to have to confess this to you but I never learned how to do any real baking other than breads."

"But all the wonderful deserts you serve with your great meals." LaRae was dumfounded over Shirley's confession.

"I bought them, fresh every morning, from the local bakery shop."

She stated turning to place a pan of biscuits in the oven, and then taking the tail of the apron she had on and wiped the sweat from her face.

LaRae observed the concerned look on Shirley's face. "What's wrong?"

"I heard this morning that the proprietor of the bakery shop, Mr. Abraham, his wife, Helen, had a heart attack day before yesterday and the shop will be closing for awhile."

"Were you close friends with the Abrahams?" LaRae was concerned for her friend.

"Not close friends, but I know them and they are good folks." Shirley hesitated before speaking once more. "I know this sounds really bad but—the bakery shop will be closed and I'll have no bake goods to serve for the holiday."

LaRae couldn't hide the pleasure on her face. "If that's all that has you troubled I can fix your problem for you." She smiled at Shirley. "My grandmother taught me how to bake and I love doing it." She turned to face her friend. "You cook the holiday meal and I'll do all the baking for you. You'll just have to tell me what deserts you want to go with your meal."

Shirley looked at her with amazement. "You mean to tell me all this time you've had this talent and have been hiding it from me."

"No, I thought you did your own baking, just as you did all your own cooking." Shirley instantly saw the defensive walls go up around her young friend. "Oh, Baby Doll you had better believe I will be putting your talent to good use around here, no more shop bought bake goods in this kitchen." Smiling, she hugged her young friend close.

"What do you want to bake for desert to go with this evening's meal? I'm baking a pot roast with all the fixings."

LaRae entered the pantry and looked around at the supplies on hand. "Do you have fresh cream?" She called out to Shirley. "Yes, two pints," Shirley responded. "How about a peach cobbler made with the fresh peaches you put up last summer?" "That sounds delicious." Shirley's mouth watered at the thought of it.

It was Christmas Eve night and the aroma of LaRae's two days of baking still lingered in the air. She had baked a red velvet cake; fudge squares, brownies, and a chocolate pie on the first day. On the second day she baked a carrot cake, her own special recipe for holiday cookies, plus a pecan, and pumpkin pies. Shirley having a hard time keeping the men out of the cakes and pies that were special for the Christmas dinner; gave in and allowed them to have their choice of the deserts with their coffee this night in the parlor. To watch them in the kitchen, one would have thought they were young boys let loose in a candy store. The women giggled at their actions; the way they playfully pushed and shoved each other out of the way and took forkfuls off one another's plate was amusing.

Hearing no sound in the now quite house, LaRae silently slipped from her room with her wrapped gifts and now-stuffed stockings in hand headed in the direction of the parlor. Upon entering the parlor, LaRae was taken aback at the silhouette of a man standing near the Christmas tree.

"It's me, Jason." He should have realized she might be startled. "Don't be alarmed."

She stopped in front of the fireplace and stood there, barefoot, in nightgown and loose robe. The light from the fireplace turned her tumble of long blond curls into a halo surrounding her now pale face. "I didn't know anyone was still up," her voice was a little shaky.

Crossing the room to join her, he reached for the packages in her hands. "I was just doing a little reminiscing of Christmases past." He placed the nicely wrapped gifts under the tree. LaRae placed the stocking she had made for each friend on top of the gift she had bought them.

"Good night, sorry I disturbed your visit in the past. I hope they were good memories"

"They were—warm ones of Christmases when my parents were alive—most of them here in this house with Aunt Shirley and Uncle Jacob. We always celebrated Christmas with them. We would arrive a week before Christmas, which would give enough time for the men to find just the right tree and for mama and Aunt Shirley to do all the baking and cooking." LaRae could see the smile on his face from where she stood. She quietly slipped out of the room, allowing Jason his private stroll down memory lane this night.

Just as the sun was rising LaRae pulled the rocking chair back away from the fireplace and put the folded quilt in its place at the foot of the bed. Today would be a busy day; it was Christmas. She dressed in black slacks with a mustard yellow sweater over a black turtleneck and a pair of black boots. After braiding her hair and twisting it on top of her head and securing it in place with a comb, she left her room for the kitchen.

Shirley was already in the kitchen busy with preparing breakfast when LaRae entered. "Anything I can do to help." She went straight to the drawer and removed an apron and tied it around her waist.

"Check on the biscuits in the oven, I think their ready to come out." Shirley removed the cast iron skillet from the stove and poured the contents of sausage gravy into a bowel. "You take this and I'll get the milk and butter and be right behind you." Shirley handed LaRae the bowl of gravy along with the plate of biscuits then turned to get the butter and milk before following her into the dinning room.

At five o'clock, for Christmas celebration, LaRae had changed into an emerald green velvet dress with a pointed collar of white lace. The long tapered sleeves had white lace peeking out at the wrist. The midi length skirt of the dress was gathered at the waist. She wore a pair of emerald green velvet flats. Her hair was pulled up on the sides with gold combs and hanging loose in the back.

Everyone had already assembled in the parlor when she entered the room and seated herself at her usual place beside the hearth. Shirley had moved a table into the far corner and after adorning it with a table cloth, placed bake goods, sandwiches, chips and dips, along with a coffee pot and a punch bowl of eggnog upon it. They had the traditional breakfast that morning followed by their Christmas dinner at noon; and now they were gathered in the parlor for a light meal and the exchanging of gifts.

The day ended too soon and now LaRae was alone in her room with the gifts her friends had given her placed on her bed to be put away. Mr. Potts had given her a pair of brown leather gloves with a dark blue scarf; Professor Cove gave her an antique crystal perfume bottle, which he found in a small local shop. She removed the gloves and scarf from their box and placed them with her coat that hung on a peg by the door. Afterwards she carefully removed the crystal perfume bottle from its container and placed it on the dresser among her collection of different fragrances.

Jason had given her a gold chain with a beautiful gold cross pendent hanging from it; Shirley gave her a black leather bound Bible with her name engraved in gold lettering on the front cover of it. With care she removed the necklace from the small package and positioned it around her neck then walked over to the mirror and looked at her reflection. Her last gift after opening the box she folded back the tissue paper and removed from the package the Bible her friend had given her. She run her fingers gently across the gold lettering, and then placed the book on the table beside the fireplace where she pulled up the rocking chair every night.

LaRae, as she did every night, positioned the rocker in front of the fireplace beside the small table that now held the Bible her friend had given her for Christmas. Even though she didn't understand it, she had started reading the Bible out loud every night to drown out James' voice with its evil assault on her mind and emotions. She would read until dawn hoping she would not fall asleep during the night hours.

CHAPTER 8

LaRae awoke with a jerk and found herself in an almost pitch dark room and painfully sore from slipping into an awkward position in the rocking chair in her sleep. Instinctively, she didn't move. Holding herself very still, she listened intently, trying to decide what had awakened her.

Sleep had become a luxury; she'd discovered that long ago. She'd been afraid to be alone in the darkness; nightmares kept her awake, sometimes for days and weeks at a time. If she dozed off, terrible images filled her head growing out of her imagination, her memory, and her fear. She'd forced herself to stay awake to avoid the horror of her subconscious mind.

Holding her breath, she listened intensely; half-afraid she would hear someone else's breathing in the room with her. Yet, very afraid she would feel someone reach out and grab her if she didn't move, her survival instincts kicked in instantly. Easing ever so slowly from the chair she crept gradually in the dark to the lamp beside the bed and turned it on. The light, blinding at first, revealed she was the only occupant of the room.

What bothered LaRae the most was her inability to explain the sound she knew she heard. After drawing up all her courage, she searched the room and adjoining bath thoroughly and found nothing that could have roused her from her restless sleep. There were no open windows—and with it being winter—no stray four-legged creatures scurrying around or taking up residence in a nook or cranny.

No logical explanation at all.

"Except it's finally happened," she said out loud. "I've gone crazy. Why can't I just admit it to myself?"

She looked down at her hands not surprised to see them shaking. Was she really going crazy?

"I can't tell," she muttered wearily, raking her hands through her long, blond hair.

She sat in the rocker and willed herself to breath evenly, to quiet her pounding heart and empty her mind of the nightmarish images that assailed her. It took a long time to calm down. When she felt steady enough to move, she built up the fire that had burned down to hot coals in the fireplace then took her place once more in the rocker. There, she heard no more sounds, nor did the nightmares intrude again. She picked up the Bible from its place on the table beside the rocker, opened it, and started to read. She rationalized, if she stayed awake, she couldn't dream.

She dozed off once, and then quickly awoke again around dawn. Working the kinks out of her stiff limbs, LaRae dressed for the morning in jeans and a dark blue sweater. She welcomed the peace of the morning. The dawning light seemed to wash away her bad dreams. After pulling her hair back in a long plat, she walked to the kitchen.

"Good morning," Shirley greeted, unable to hide her concern as LaRae entered the kitchen.

"Good morning," LaRae responded in as cheerful a voice as she could muster up. Noticing the coffee pot was almost empty she asked, "Is it still hot?"

"Should be, I was just fixing to make some fresh."

"I'll do it." LaRae said pouring the last of the dark liquid into her cup.

After preparing the pot for another making of the fresh dark liquid brew, LaRae climbed onto a stool on the opposite side of the bar, where Shirley was preparing breakfast, intent on enjoying her cup of coffee.

Noticing the obvious dark circles under her friend's eyes and pale complexion, Shirley asked. "Are you feeling well?"

"I didn't sleep well last night," LaRae replied weakly.

LaRae got down off the stool despite a headache and sore muscles and putting on an apron helped Shirley finish with the last preparation for breakfast. She wanted to avoid any conversation with her friend, even though she knew it was out of true concern. After placing the meal on the table so the men could eat and be off to their endeavors, she once more retreated to her room. This had become her routine not long after Christmas. Here it was the middle of February and everything was getting worse in her coping with the horrors of the past James left her with, instead of better.

She not only was withdrawing from her friends but also from herself. Each day she withdrew deeper and deeper within herself to the point she found she had neither feelings nor emotions. She was finding it hard to even pretend around her friends, she therefore had chosen to retreat to her room. The room she hated to be alone in—the room full of nightmares, night hour demons, and James' voice—now was a hiding place from the people she truly craved to be with. Yet, she just wanted to be alone.

She knew staying away from her friends was causing them great concern and she wouldn't do anything in the world to hurt them. It's just right now she didn't have the strength to pretend everything was good with her—and fight her demons too. LaRae fought the only way she knew how; she stayed awake at night, taking very short naps during the day. To drown out James' voice she would softly talk or read out loud to herself. For her to banish the demons that hid in the shadows of her room, she would leave a dim light on at nighttime.

With each day that passed, LaRae had become more and more withdrawn—even to the point that she quit taking her meals with the group. She just wanted to be alone. So each morning, even though winter still held its icy grip on the area, she would sneak out of the house before anyone was up and about and drive her vehicle to a local park. At the park she would spend the day feeding the birds and walking some of the shorter nature trails. It was still a little difficult for her to get around because of her knee, but she managed herself well with the help of a cane. After walking, she would set in her automobile—while consuming a thermos of hot chocolate bought at a local diner—and warm up by enjoying the view of the mountains while watching the town's people come and go about their daily routine.

After drinking her last cup of hot chocolate, she looked at her watch, shifted her vehicle into drive and eased it out onto the side road. She marveled at the picturesque view of the landscape between town and the *Bed & Breakfast*. The beautiful snowcapped mountains against a clear blue sky, peaking over the naked treetops, was a scene that would rival any in a nature magazine.

LaRae knew Shirley's everyday habits in detail. The time was one o'clock. After cleaning up from the noon meal, her friend would usually lie-down for a short nap; this would be a perfect time for LaRae to slip back into the house and into her room unobserved.

She silently entered her room. At once, LaRae closed the door behind her. Her stomach churned, and she found she was trembling as she stepped back from the door. She half turned away, angry and disgusted with herself. "You're not as tough as you pretend to be," she snapped. She was shaking inside.

LaRae walked to the rocking chair and despairingly eased herself down into it then begins to slowly move it backward and forward. Leaning her head against the back of the chair, she allowed the tears, which had gathered, in her eyes to flow freely down her cheeks. "I give up—I give up!" She cried faintly. "I have no more strength to fight what I can't see. How can I fight someone that's dead—dead and buried? I can't run because you're always there with me where ever I go—in my mind and in my dreams—you're always there. Where can I go that you can't follow?"

LaRae must have dozed off for the next thing she heard was a light tapping on her door. "Yes, who is it?" In a shaky voice she called out.

"It's me, Shirley. Are you coming for supper?"

"No, thanks. I'm-I'm not really hungry." She replied through the closed door.

LaRae noticed all her muscles were tense and she had been holding her breath. After a few minutes of taking slow deep breaths, her breathing was once more calm. She soaked in a hot bath to relax her tight muscles. If she thought the hot bath would calm her nerves or mask the voice in her mind, she was sadly mistaken. She didn't know how much longer she could go on like this.

"Are you loosing your mind? Are you really crazy after all?" She questioned her own sanity. That was her biggest fear, she supposed. Going really crazy, that the bonds of reason might snap inside of her and she would be gone forever. It could happen, she knew. She had patients before with posttraumatic stress disorder. Of course most of them were veterans, but could it happen to anyone?

LaRae lost track of the days, for she was to the point where she never left her room. She would sit in her room day and night in the old rocking chair gently rocking back and forth and softly crying. She had not only given up fighting what she feared the most but also given up on trying to drown out James' voice. He controlled her every move when he was alive, why shouldn't he control her every thought when he's dead?

Night had fallen yet again on the town. The dim light mixed with the light from the fire washed LaRae's room in an amber glow that didn't quite reach the far corners. The only noise heard in the room was the low rhythmic back and forth sound of the rocker.

Almost in an total hypnotic state, LaRae slowly rising from the rocker, walked to the bathroom, opened the medicine cabinet and removed the unused bottle of pain medication, which had been prescribed for her after her knee replacement surgery. Upon reentering the room she walked over to the bedside table picked up the pitcher of water and filled the glass sitting next to it. After making herself comfortable on the right side of the bed, LaRae picked the bottle of pills up in her hand and looked at it. Quickly dropping the bottle back on to the bed, she placed her hands over her ears and began shaking her head back and forth.

"No, no, no," she cried. "Leave me alone. Why won't you just leave me alone?" LaRae fell back on the pillows and wept silently.

A short time later, as if under a spell LaRae quickly sat up and in one fluid motion picked up the bottle of pills, removed the cap and poured them out on the bed in front of her. Looking at the pills she picked one up then put it in her mouth; with the water glass in hand she took a drink. LaRae repeated the sequence of taking a pill then taking a drink of water three times. Suddenly the television set in her room, which she never watched, came on all by itself and begin flipping through the channels. Unable to find the remote to turn it off, she turned it off the old fashion way, by hand.

Settled on the bed—yet again—with all the pills she could find in her left hand, LaRae reached for the water glass. Simultaneously as she reached for the water glass, the television set once more came on, flipped through the channels, and then stopped on a channel where an older man was talking to a large group of people inside of a big tent about a man named Jesus. Suddenly, he turned and pointed his finger at her and said, "Young lady sitting there with a handful of pills contemplating suicide, Jesus wants you to know he loves you. You think you're loosing your mind that you're going crazy—that no one loves you. I want you to know that you're not—you're under demonic attack. Put those pills down. Jesus loves you. Do you hear me? He loves you." Just as sudden as it came on the television set went off.

The room now quiet, the only sound heard was her own ragged breathing and the pounding of her heart in her ears. She looked at the pills in her hand; promptly walking to the bathroom she flushed them down the toilet. After gagging herself to try and get rid of as much of the pills as she could of what she had already taken, she washed her face then turned out the bathroom light. Once more she eased herself into the rocker and started to cry.

She didn't want to die; she just wanted James to leave her alone. She just wanted to have a life. Was she going crazy? Was she supposed to die now because she didn't die back then like James had been telling her? These thoughts continued to go over and over in her mind.

"I need help. I can't do this anymore. Sooner or later you're going to kill me. I don't have the strength to fight you anymore." LaRae spoke softly to the ceiling.

No more had LaRae spoken those words and she heard a soft knock on her door. "Who is it?" she whispered.

"It's me, Shirley! May I come in?"

LaRae hesitated for only a moment before answering. "Yes, please do."

Shirley opened the door, walked over to where her friend sat in the rocking chair, eased her up to a standing position, and wrapped her arms around her hugging her close. The tears starting all over again as Shirley lead LaRae to the foot of the bed where they sat down beside each other.

"It's time to talk. You can't keep on like this." Shirley tenderly told LaRae while gently holding her hands. "I've been praying everyday and every night for you, tonight the Lord told me it was time and sent me to you."

"Tonight?" LaRae looked astonished.

"Yes. Why?"

"Because something happened tonight that's hard even for me to believe and it happened to me."

"What happened?" Shirley already knew something had changed in the spiritual realm. She had been in spiritual warfare for a long time over her friend and tonight she felt a release.

LaRae eased off the bed and started to pace the floor keeping her gaze on the flooring before her never once looking Shirley in the face as she recounted the night's events to her friend. She told about feeling like she was under a spell almost dream-like and too weak to fight, about taking the pills, then the televisions set coming on, and unable to find the remote; and finally having to switch it off by hand. LaRae paused waiting for Shirley's reaction. After not getting one she then continued and told of flushing the pills. She picked up the story relating all the events ending with the words the man on the T.V. had said and how she felt he was talking directly to her. When she finished with her story she set down in the rocking chair, and looked at her friend directly in the face for the first time.

"He was you know," Shirley paused for a moment. "And he does you know."

"What are you talking about?" LaRae was obviously confused.

"The man on the T.V. was talking directly to you. God showed you to him at that moment in time then he had his angels turn on the T.V. so you could hear that minister tell you how much Jesus loves you."

Now LaRae was even more confused than before. "How can God do something like that?"

"Because God is omnipotent, omnipresent, and omniscient, that means He has unlimited power. He can be everywhere at the same time, and he has complete knowledge and awareness of what's going on. He could see you here in this room in the state of mind you where in and under the attack you were under; then speak to the man on the T.V. where he was at the same time. The reason He spoke to the man on the T.V. was because of His great love for you."

"I just don't understand how He could." LaRae said and wanting to believe in something as strongly as her friend did. Shirley, along with her family and friends, attended church services on Sundays. At every meal, those gathered around Shirley's dining table would hear her or Jason ask God's blessing over the food and over all of those in attendance. Her friends would always tell her it wasn't religion it was relationship. She didn't understand the difference, even though she wanted to.

"Where is your Bible?" Shirley looked around the room. "If you'll get it I can show you."

LaRae picked up the leather bound book off the table beside the rocking chair and walked over to where Shirley sat on the bed.

"I've been reading in it." LaRae flipped open the book to where the bookmarker was slightly sticking out of the book. "I'm reading about Moses, here's where I am on chapter twenty." LaRae looked at her friend a little bewildered. "Maybe this book will mean to me what it means to you the more I read—but right now it is just stories about people—I want it to be more." LaRae hesitated then looked at her friend before saying anymore. "I want what you and the others have. You told me you draw your strength from this book." Tears had begun to gather in LaRae's eyes and roll down her checks as she spoke to her friend.

Taking the book from LaRae, Shirley patted the bed beside her for her friend to sit down. As soon as LaRae eased down on the bed beside her, Shirley opened the book. After flipping through the pages, she pointed to a verse. "We're going to start with Romans chapter three verse twenty-three. I want you to read this verse."

LaRae began reading from where Shirley was pointing. "For all have sinned, and come short of the glory of God;"

"Now let us go to First John chapter one verse ten and you read."

"If we say we have not sinned, we make him a liar, and his word is not in us."

In a soft voice Shirley started to explain the verses to LaRae, "According to what you just read we are all sinners and have come short of the glory of God and if we say we haven't sinned we call God a liar. That means every humanbeing on this earth is a sinner. We have all sinned and disappointed God because of our sin. We were born sinners. There is an age of accountability when you grow to know right from wrong—sin from righteousness and you will have to make a choice. Everyone has to make a choice." LaRae just listened to her friend's explanation, even though she already had many questions.

"Now let us go to Romans chapter five verse eight and you read."

"But God commendeth his love toward us, in that, while we were yet sinners, Christ died for us."

Shirley taking the book once more from her friend flipped through the pages. "Here we go the Gospel of John chapter three; start reading here at verse sixteen through to seventeen."

"For God so loved the world that he gave his only begotten Son, that whosoever believeth in him should not perish, but have everlasting life. For God sent not his Son into the world to condemn the world; but that the world through him might be saved."

As with the previous verves Shirley explained there had to be a sacrifice for sin, not only for her sins but also for everybody's sins, which Christ Jesus, God's only begotten Son, chose to be. Shirley reminded LaRae of her own Bible reading about the animal sacrifices the Jewish leaders had to make for the people.

Before leaving the room Shirley handed LaRae a piece of paper upon which she had written a few other verses she wanted LaRae to read.

"Also read the four Gospels they are the first four books of the New Testament. They tell the story of Jesus—I believe reading them will be helpful for your understanding of who He is and what He did for us." Shirley left the room quietly closing the door behind her.

LaRae would never have dreamed come Sunday morning she would find herself searching through the closet to find something appropriate to wear to church. Why had she accepted Shirley's invitation to go with the small group today, when she hadn't attended church since she was very young?

When she finished dressing and took a look in the full-length mirror on the closet door, LaRae decided she look acceptable. Shirley had said the church was a small country church so she selected something not too sophisticated. She wore an ankle length black pleated skirt topped with a black jacket. The scoop-necked silk blouse was an ivory color that blended gracefully with her pearl like complexion; she then paired black pumps with the outfit. She wore her long blond hair braided then twisted into a type of bun high on the back of her head. Picking up the leather bound Bible Shirley had given her, LaRae left the room, softly closing the door behind her.

"Good morning." Shirley greeted as LaRae entered the room.

"Good morning." The men echoed

"Good morning. Have I kept y'all waiting long?" She asked noticing everyone assembled for coffee and waiting in the parlor.

"Not at all, we still have over half an hour before services begin—and it's only a fifteen minute drive to the church."

"Shall we go then?" Jason asked finishing his coffee a few minutes later and placing the empty cup on the table.

'Yes," Shirley said. "I don't see why not. LaRae can sit in the front seat with you Jason and Mr. Potts, Professor Cove, and I will sit in the back"

LaRae's mind drifted in many different directions but she soon reeled it in when she noticed Jason, who sat beside her, maneuvering the car onto a rocky driveway. The name of the church on an old paint-chipped sign read *Believer's Victory Church* as they drove past it to a small wooden church building. According to the sign over the door, the church had been built in 1900. LaRae walked between Jason and Shirley up the center aisle into the small sanctuary followed by Mr. Potts and Professor Cove.

Shirley handed LaRae a hymnal when the minister announced the first song. It was a song she didn't know, but she followed the words on the page as she listened to Shirley's strong soprano voice blending with Jason's alto voice. Remembering that James had told her at one time she sounded like a croaking frog when she tried to sing, LaRae sang softly, not much over a whisper, on the following two songs.

The minister, Malachi Jenkins, was a humble, medium-built, middle-aged man, but he was sincere and his obvious knowledge held LaRae's attention. She listened eagerly to every word as he started his sermon.

According to the Minister, there was a ruler of the Jewish people named Nicodemus. Knowing the Pharisees and Jewish ruler wanted to kill Jesus; Nicodemus believed in him and would come to Jesus by night to learn from him. Jesus told Nicodemus, unless a man is born again, he cannot see the kingdom of God. Nicodemus was confused and wanted to know how a man could be born when he is old? How could he enter his mother's womb for a second time to be born again?

Intrigued by this subject that was important to her, LaRae listened intently when Minister Jenkins read a few more verses from the Bible, giving the third chapter of John as reference.

"Verily, verily I say unto thee, except a man be born of water and of the Spirit, he cannot enter into the kingdom of God. That which is born of the flesh is flesh; and that which is born of the Spirit is spirit."

The minister used many of the verses that Shirley had showed her several nights ago. As the minister continued with his message quoting verse after verse about God's love, something started taking place with her. LaRae felt a yearning—a pulling inside of her she could not explain.

By the time the minister asked the congregation to stand for the invitation tears were rolling down her cheeks and her whole body quivered uncontrollably. The soft musical notes of the organ, played by Pastor Jenkins' wife, mixed in harmony with the angelic voices of the congregation, pulled her toward the alter in front of the sanctuary.

LaRae felt Shirley's arm gently wrap around her shoulder and hold her close.

"Jesus loves you. You do know that don't you?" Shirley softly whispered. LaRae couldn't answer for the crying so she just nodded her head in an affirmative response. "Don't you think it's time you meet him?" Again LaRae shook her head in response to her question.

Shirley, taking the younger girl by the hand, led her from their seats. Together they walked down the aisle to the church alter. Immediately LaRae fell to her knees and poured out her heart to the Lord Jesus. After many tears of repentance and a washing by the Lord, LaRae raised from her kneeling position a new person. Alive in Christ just as the Bible had said she would be.

LaRae had her hand shook by most of the congregation at the end of the service along with many invitations to become a part of their fellowship. After the crowd had dwindled some, Minister Jenkins invited her to a Bible class he and his wife, Ella, taught on Friday nights for newborn believers. It was a small group consisting of eight baby newcomers to the Lord.

The Minister explained that in these classes they taught on the subjects that were important for new believers. The most important one was the reading of the Bible and where to start with their reading. He also taught on the importance of prayer, fasting and tithing—to name just a few things. He believed this was important knowledge that a new believer needed to help them stay consistent in their walk with God and not fall by the wayside. After leaving the church, LaRae made up her mind to attend the classes and would let the minister know before next week's service.

On the trip home LaRae felt as if she were lightheaded—floating and totally filled—saturated with pure love. It was so hard for her to explain what she was feeling—to even try and put it into words was impossible.

Upon arriving home, she quickly changed into jeans and a sweater and then hurried into the kitchen to help Shirley with the noon meal. She had so many questions to ask her friend, yet she had no idea where to even begin.

As she rounded the corner to the kitchen she was greeted with a wonderful heartfelt welcome. "Hello, Sister Jones," the whole group greeted. "It's so wonderful to see you." Each member of the group took turns greeting her with hugs and kisses on the cheeks. She was passed back and forth between them time and time again. Yet, LaRae knew the feelings she felt from her friends were genuine.

"You know you're not only our friend, but also our sister in Christ now." Shirley said as she hugged her close once more.

CHAPTER 9

The next few days, LaRae quickly adapted to her new role in life. She slept for the first time in her bed—instead of the rocking chair—and sat often in the garden gazebo meditating. She walked about the grounds every day. She spent a lot of time reading her Bible, basking in God's love for her. She memorized a verse from the book of First John. "God is love. Whoever lives in love lives in God, and God in him."

She considered herself patiently waiting on spring's arrival. Yet, one day as she and Shirley walked around the grounds, her patience about worn thin, asked, "Where is spring? Has it gotten lost somewhere?"

Shirley laughingly responded. "Remember God is always in control."

"Spring time is a special time of the year to me. It's a time of new life; a time when the silence of the morning is broken by the hungry chirping of newborn baby birds."

The two women entered the gazebo and sat down. LaRae pulled a plastic bag from under her chair, opened it and removed two crocheted blankets. She handed one to Shirley and kept one for herself. Shirley looked at her curiously as she took the blanket and wrapped it about her.

"I made them during the nights I couldn't sleep and brought them out here to help keep me warm." LaRae felt she had to defend her actions.

"Good idea," Shirley responded. "Even though the sun's out, the temperature is still cold." She pulled the blanket higher up around her shoulders.

"I know. I keep waiting for spring to make its appearance," LaRae responded as Shirley watched her face take on a heavenly glow as she thought of the spring time season.

"Tell me why spring is so special to you."

"I love the anticipation of waiting for the appearance of the first robin of the year, watching for the first buds to form on the trees and plants." LaRae stood up and walked to the front of the gazebo and looked out as she continued talking. "Spring is seeing the snow slowly melt and watching the frozen ground become a mass of mud, then suddenly turn into a carpet of bright green grass. It's the thrill of finding the first crocus as it pushes its way through the last remains of old man winter's snow. It's feeling the warmth of the wind as it softly touches my face." She turned around and faced Shirley. "And now that I'm a Christian and have learned the real meaning, it's Easter—Resurrection—a promise of a new beginning. It's a season full of promises."

Shirley rose from her seat and placed her arm around the younger woman's waist. "When you say it like that how can spring not be everybody's favorite season?" The two women walked back toward the house arm in arm.

Supper was over, the dishes were cleared and the group had gathered as they always had in the parlor for coffee and conversation. LaRae, sitting in her usual place beside the hearth, waited until after the small talk had died down for the night before making her announcement. "At the end of the month I'll be moving back into my own home." She waited a moment before going on. By this time she had everyone's full attention. "I've already called my attorney and he's making all the arrangements for me."

"But, why?" Shirley begins but couldn't finish the sentence. She knew LaRae was on her way to recovery, physically. It was her emotional state Shirley was worried about. She was healing since starting her walk with the Lord. Yet, she just wasn't where she needed to be emotionally. "I know, Lord, I put her in your hands and I have to trust you to take care of her." She silently prayed.

"It's time for me to go home; to the home I told you my Great Aunt Kate left me. I'm ready to make a fresh start on my own." She looked at Shirley. "It's not like I'm moving out of state or something." She laughed to change the mood in the room. "I'll drop by often and I'll see you at church."

"Just make sure you bring a supply of desert when you come." Jason chimed in causing the whole group to laugh.

*

Moving day came too quickly for LaRae, but she was glad to be back in her own home once more. She awoke early to the harmony of birds singing outside her bedroom window. Spring had finally come and she was so excited. She was starting a new life. A new life without fears—without nightmares—without demons hiding in the dark.

She threw back the coverlet and excitedly jumped out of bed. Walking to the closet and finding her robe, she opened the bedroom door. She started down the hall toward the kitchen; the hardwood floors cool against her bare feet. Coffee and breakfast were the first things on her mind before tackling the last of her unpacking.

She walked among the many boxes that remained on her living room floor that she needed to go through and decide where to put the contents of each. Her friends had helped earlier in the week with the placement of the furniture and heavier items. Her excursion through the boxes was interrupted by the ringing of the front door bell. She placed her half emptied cup of coffee on an end table and proceeded to answer the front door.

"Who could that be at this time of the morning?" Wondering as she unlocked the bolt on the front door.

"Am I in time for coffee?" Shirley gaily chirped. Not waiting for an invitation she gave LaRae a quick hug and headed for the kitchen.

"Yes, please come in." Glad to see her friend, LaRae closed the door and retrieved her cup of coffee from the end table and followed Shirley into the kitchen. Entering the kitchen she noticed Shirley had filled a cup with coffee and had already taken a seat at the table. "How have you been?" LaRae asked as she poured a fresh cup of coffee for herself then sat down at the table opposite of Shirley.

"I just stopped by to see if you needed any help with the rest of your unpacking and invite you to supper tonight."

"You've done enough already—I can't ask you..."

Shirley quickly interrupted her. "You're not asking I'm offering."

"Alright, you win." LaRae looked at her friend before continuing. "The Lord has been dealing with me about accepting help from others instead of trying to always do things on my own."

"Great. Where do I start?" Shirley asked enthusiastic over LaRae's change of heart.

"Let me get changed into something more suitable for working." Grinning, she looked down at the robe and gown she was wearing.

LaRae soon emerged from her bedroom dressed in lightly faded jeans and pale blue chambray shirt to find Shirley hard at work unpacking a large box of books. LaRae watched for a few minutes as her friends neatly dusted then placed each book on the oak shelves of the bookcases to the left side of the fireplace.

"Are you going to watch all day or work?" Shirley jokingly asked.

"You were doing such a good job I thought I would just watch and learn."

"Yeah, sure. Ms. Neat as a pin is going to learn something from her disorderly friend. That'll be the day." Shirley laughingly responded and threw the dust cloth at LaRae. The jubilant atmosphere of joking and teasing continued the rest of the day between the two women as they worked together.

With the day's unpacking completed the women drove back to the *Bed & Breakfast* where LaRae would help Shirley prepare supper for the night. She brought with her a surprise of three pies she had prepared the night before with intentions of dropping them off today. The pies were a thank you gift for her friends for all their hard work and help they had given her.

The conversation in the parlor was about the visiting minister, Evangelist Paul Toby, which Pastor Jenkins had invited for Sunday's service. No one in the group had heard him minister, personally, but Pastor Jenkins spoke very highly of him.

"I'm looking forward to hearing him speak. I've heard his sermons are very powerful," Professor Cove added to the conversation while cutting a piece of pie.

"I ran into Sister Jenkins at the diner yesterday and she told me this evangelist has been known to be used by the Lord in word of knowledge and prophecy too." Mr. Potts added.

Shirley drained the last of her coffee and said, "Well, Pastor Jenkins did say he was a humble unpretentious man. That's all God's looking for in a vessel." Sitting quietly, LaRae listened intently to the conversation surrounding the visiting evangelist. She was looking forward to the service and hearing the minister for herself.

Sunday morning dawned a beautiful spring morning. This was the morning LaRae had looked forward to with great anticipation; it's not that she didn't look forward to every church service, but this one was special. The visiting minister, Evangelist Paul Toby, would be ministering in this Sunday service.

She wore a pale blue lightweight gauzy wrap-around ankle length dress with elbow-length loose flowing sleeves and white sandals with a one-inch heel. Her long blond hair was pulled back from her face with a small white bow and then allowed to hang loosely down her back. The only jewelry that adorned her outfit was a pale blue ribbon choker trimmed in tiny white lace.

LaRae arrived in the *Believer's Victory Church* parking lot the same time as her friends. They walked across the parking lot chatting about the week's events. Entering the sanctuary together the group took their usual seats and awaited the beginning of the services.

Pastor Jenkins opened the service and made all the needed announcements. After leading the congregations in a couple of hymnals, he introduced Evangelist Toby.

Evangelist Toby started his message by telling the congregation, "We know that we can receive two different types of wounds, Physical wounds that wound our physical man; and emotional wounds that wound our soul man." He then gave Scripture references. First he read from the book First Peter chapter two, "*Who his own self bare our sins in His own body on the tree, which we, being dead to sin, should live unto righteousness: by whose stripes ye were healed.*" Then he gave Psalm chapter thirty-four verse eighteen, "*The Lord is nigh unto them that are of a broken heart.*" Then he told us Psalm one hundred and forty-seven verse three tells us… "*He healeth the broken in heart, bindedth up their wounds.*"

Paul Toby paused and looked at the congregation before speaking again. "Remember the old childhood saying, '*sticks and stones may break my bones but words can never harm me*'. This is a lie! A lie straight from the father of all lies! We all know that words can hurt. No, they don't leave physical wounds for all to see but words do leave wounds on the inside of us, wounds that affect our soul man. I call these wounds heart pains."

The anointed words flowed from the evangelist. "Heart pains hurt us just as seriously as physical pains do, maybe even more, because it takes much longer for us to heal from our heart pains than it does to heal from physical wounds. Sometimes, we keep these hurts locked up or buried so deep inside of us that we never get over these pains." LaRae was overwhelmed by the evangelist's words. According to him LaRae had heart pains.

LaRae listened intently as Evangelist Toby continued. "Jesus took the stripes on His back so we could be healed from not only physical wounds but also of emotional wounds. For those who may not believe healing is for today, then let it be known that God allowed His dear Son,

Jesus, to be beaten for nothing. When the Bible tells us By His stripes we were healed, it is not just talking about physical wounds that are on the outside for all to see; but it is also talking about the heart wounds we carry deep inside of us that no one but God can see. Our Father sees us from the inside out. He sees our soul man. He sees all the hurting, bleeding wounds our soul man has sustained; wounds that were caused by others with their careless words."

By this time, Paul Toby had left the pulpit area and began to walk back and forth in front of the alter as he continued with his message. "This is why God tells us in Proverbs the eighteenth chapter and twenty-first verse that we hold the power of life and death, blessing, and cursing in our tongue. The words that come out of our mouth can build someone up or tear someone down. The words we speak should bless, build-up, encourage, gladden, or give confidence to others. But instead, most of the time, the words that come out of our mouths hurt, rip-up, or sadden others—causing heart pains. The reason the wounds hurt us so bad and are hard to get over is because they are caused by people that we trust, people that are suppose to love us, not hurt us. People like mothers, fathers, brothers, sisters, husbands, wives, aunts, uncles even our best friends."

LaRae felt as though she was the only person in the church and Evangelist Toby was ministering just to her. Every time he spoke she felt a quickening inside of her soul. She had been hurting for a very long time. She concentrated on the words Evangelist Toby was speaking.

Paul Toby looked at each person in the congregation to reassure them before speaking. "God not only wants to heal your physical pains that affect your physical man, but He, also, especially wants to heal your emotional pains that affect your soul man. Many of you carry around heart wounds with you today that occurred many years ago. These wounds still mold and shape you and control you even today. These wounds have made you who you are. Because of these wounds your past is dictating your future."

He pointed a finger at different ones in the congregation and said.

"Every person in this room was created for a purpose. And if you were created for a purpose then you have a vision from God to accomplish that purpose. That purpose is what most people call—your calling. There are so very many of God's children that are not walking in their calling, because they are stuck in their past. Their past is controlling them. Every choice they make today is based on their past. You cannot walk toward your vision when you're being controlled by your past. Jesus tells us in Luke chapter nine… *'No man, having put his hand to the plow, and looking back, is fit for the kingdom of God'.* God wants to heal you. It is time for you to get rid of those pains that have been controlling your lives all this time."

Evangelist Toby stopped center of the alter and looked at the congregations. "God wants to heal your soul man of all its open hurting wounds. He wants to apply His healing balm to every wound. It's time you stop letting the pains of your past dictate your present and your future."

Walking up and down the aisle he asked. "Don't you think these pains have controlled you and your life long enough? Then he made a bold statement. "It's time to say enough is enough! It's time to let go of the past! You can't walk in your future until you let go of your past!"

Many members of the congregation, with tears on their cheeks, went forward to be prayed for by Evangelist Toby. Some of the older women that had gone forward to be prayed for had hidden their pain for many years. They had suffered in silence.

After praying for the members that had come forward, Paul Toby walked among the congregation stopping and speaking over different members with a Word of Knowledge God had gifted him with. He stopped beside the pew where LaRae sat between Jason and Shirley. He pointed toward her and asked if she would step out into the aisle.

"You have been having a dream," he begin, "you're standing outside of a home and you're entrance is blocked by a large iron rusty gate with a chain and padlock securing it closed. In this dream you see that the home has long been closed up. The plant life surrounding the house is dead and decaying and the once charming structure that now stood in ruins is only a shadow of what it use to be. As you look around, you see nothing but death all around this house. Everywhere you look, everything is deteriorating and decaying."

She begins to tremble as he recites her dream back to her. LaRae looked at him astonished that he knew about a dream she had told to no one and had held her captive for so many years. She didn't consider it a dream; it was a nightmare.

"This dream is from the Lord." He begins to tell her.

"But—but—why would…" LaRae begin because his words flabbergasted her. She wanted to know why God would want to scare her with a nightmare.

"This house is your soul man. The gate with the chain and padlock, you put up to block the entryway. The pathway leading to the house is your emotions—your feelings. He's telling you that you have locked yourself—your soul man—away so tightly you will not allow any emotions to penetrate or escape." He looked at her with such sincerity that she couldn't help but believe him. For the first time in many years she almost let her guard down.

He continued to talk to her under the anointing. "You have been hurt so deeply that for your on preservation you did the only thing you knew to do. You shut down all feeling, all caring, and all emotions." He took her hands in his. "You're not surviving, you're dieing. That was the message the Lord was showing you in the dream. You can't live without emotions. How can you feel His true love, if you won't allow feelings into your soul man?"

Tears rolled down LaRae's cheeks and she hurriedly wiped them away. "It hurts too much." She faintly told him.

"I know," he told her. He then recited part of Jeremiah chapter fifty-one verse eight. "…*take balm for her pain, if so be she may be healed.*"

LaRae listened to every word he said. She knew he was right. She had built a wall or as he said placed a locked gate around her heart. She just didn't want to be hurt anymore. Trust did not come easy for her.

"It's time for you to remove the chain and padlock to allow the Lord to throw open the gate and enter in. He will then apply His healing balm to all the open wounds your soul man has suffered over the years."

"I don't know how." She cried.

"All you have to do is open your heart up to the Lord and let Him enter in; He'll do the rest."

Evangelist Toby applied anointing oil to her forehead and said, "Be healed in Jesus' name." LaRae immediately felt an agonizing pain deep within her, so painful she doubled over in pain, unable to hold back the scream any longer; she allowed it to escape through her tight lips.

"It's okay; it will only hurt for a minute. The Lord has to dig up the painful things you have buried over the years in order to heal them."

One by one the Lord brought up each painful episode from her past. The next one more excruciating than the last until all had been taken care of by the Great Physician. LaRae felt drained yet, refreshed at the same time.

Evangelist Toby looked at her and gave her some final instructions, "You must forgive the ones that have hurt you. It will not come easy but if you be real with God and ask Him to help you, he will be faithful to help you forgive. He can put the seed of forgiveness inside of you, and then the more you pray and reinforce who you are in Christ, then the seed will take root and start to grow; before long you have a full grown plant of forgiveness blooming inside of you just bursting at the seams to come out. Then and only then will the open painful heart wounds become scars where it will become easier for you to forgive those who have hurt you and caused the devastating open wounds you have carried around inside of you for so long."

LaRae looked at the man standing in front of her scarcely able to believe her ears. How could he expect her to forgive the man who caused her so much pain—so much heartache—so much fear? She couldn't do it. She hated James for what he did to her.

Paul Toby, seeing the look of bewilderment on her face, recited from the book of Luke chapter six.

"Judge not, and ye shall not be judged: condemned not, and ye shall not be condemned: forgive, and ye shall be forgiven:"

He continued with a quote from the book of Matthew chapter five.

"But I say unto you, love your enemies, bless them that curse you, do good to them that hate you, and pray for them which despitefully use you, and persecute you."

"Right now you think there's no way you can ever forgive the one that has hurt you so badly, but if you will allow God to help you then you can. Also remember that if we don't forgive those who wronged us then God doesn't forgive us."

"I promise I'll work on it—I'd be lying to you if I told you I could forgive him right now—because I just can't—not now." LaRae slowly shook her head for emphasis.

"I know and God knows. All you have to do is ask Him for His help and He is faithful to help you."

"I will."

She took several tissues from the box on the pew in front of where she had been sitting and returned to her seat between Jason and Shirley. Pastor Jenkins repeated the announcements and dismissed the congregation.

LaRae met up with her friends at Shirley's *Bed & Breakfast* for lunch. The table was set with Shirley's famous fried chicken, mash potatoes, gravy, and corn on the cob, carrots, cornbread, and for desert peach cobbler topped with fresh cream.

"Mr. Abraham, which owns the bakery, his wife died night before last." Jason announced.

"Oh, that's so sad." LaRae stated

"She never recovered from the heart attack she had back around Christmas."

"What is he going to do now?" Shirley inquired.

"His son wants Mr. Abraham to move back to Kansas with him and his family. The Abrahams came from Kansas and his family is back there except for a daughter that lives in Iowa."

"You figure he'll sale the bakery?" LaRae asked

"That's what his son wants him to do."

"You thinking about buying the bakery?" Mr. Potts asked her as he spooned himself a second helping of peach cobbler.

"I don't know just weighing my options. I've been thinking about a change in career, about settling down in one place."

She avoided looking at any of them. She didn't want the group to know she had been thinking about this idea for a while now. She had thought about setting up a meeting with Mr. Abraham to see if he would allow her to lease the bakery while his wife was recovering. Now it was too late for that idea. But maybe she could buy the bakery and run it herself.

"Mrs. Abraham's funeral is tomorrow at two." Jason informed the group.

"Are you going?" LaRae looked at Shirley for acknowledgment.

"Yes, of course. We need to be there." Mr. Potts and Professor Cove shook their heads in agreement.

"Then I'll meet you here and ride with you, Mr. Potts, and Professor Cove."

LaRae drove home at sunset under a sky lit up with bright shades of crimson red, golden yellow, and pumpkin orange. Just to the right of her was the ball of fire dropping behind the mountain. The beauty of God's creation amazed her. She could picture God with a giant paint brush in one hand and a palette full of many colors of paints in the other, mixing the paints to get the perfect shade and then brushing the sunset before her into existence.

The next day LaRae dressed for Helen Abraham's funeral in a black midi length skirt with a matching waist length jacket and plain black pumps. A white sleeveless, round neck shell was worn underneath the jacket with no jewelry. She wore her hair pinned up under a wide brimmed black hat. After one last look in the full-length mirror on the closet door, she left the room. Picking up purse and keys off of the entryway table as she headed out of the door, she hurried to her automobile.

She drove to the *Country Living Bed & Breakfast* where she would meet up with Shirley, Mr. Potts, and Professor Cove. Entering through the back door, she poured a cup of coffee before moving ahead into the parlor. In the parlor she found the two men in friendly conversation. Both men stood and greeted her as she entered the room. Not long afterwards Shirley joined the group for short greetings before leaving for the funeral.

Mr. Potts drove to the *Bethany Church* with Shirley sitting on the front seat beside him and LaRae and Professor Cove in the back seat. The memorial service would take place inside the church and the graveside service would take place at the *Bethany Church Cemetery* beside the old church. Like the *Believer's Victory Church* this church had been standing for over a hundred years, though it had been expanded and added on to several times.

Soon after the small group returned from the funeral to the *Country Living Bed & Breakfast,* Jason showed up wanting to talk to LaRae. He invited LaRae and Shirley to meet him in the kitchen where he could talk to them in private. LaRae politely reassured him it was all right to speak in front of the others. She had grown close to her small group of friends. She, also, depended on each of the individuals to pray for her; this is why she kept the whole group informed of what's going on in her life.

"Mr. Potts and Professor Cove are a part of the group and already know a great deal about my past and they have been through many things with me, good and bad, and I have no secrets. Whatever you need to say can be voiced in front of them."

"Do you remember the private investigator, Gilbert Garth?"

"Yes, why do you ask?" Nervousness suddenly took over her body and she began to shake.

"He came to see me today."

LaRae suddenly interrupted him with questions. "What did he want—was—was he asking about me—did it have anything to do with me?"

"Calm down for just a minute and let me talk. There is nothing to be alarmed about." He calmly told her.

"Okay, you're right. James has been dead for awhile, now."

"He came to me because your ex-husband's attorneys are looking for you. It seems that you're James' only living relative and they need you to sign some papers to be able to close out his will."

"What?" LaRae was astounded. "You have got to be kidding me. That doesn't sound like James. Are you sure this isn't some kind of a trick or something?"

"I asked that very question of Mr. Garth and he said that it was all on the up and up."

"It just doesn't make any sense to me." LaRae puzzled over his words.

"All you can do is meet with them and find out what this matter is all about. If you would like I can ask Mr. Garth to make the arrangements for you to meet them at my office. I'd rather they not know where your home is located. I trust Mr. Garth I just don't trust those big city lawyers."

"I think that would be best. I can contact my attorney and have him meet us at your office on the date you set up with Mr. Garth."

CHAPTER 10

After pulling into the parking space, LaRae glanced at her watch again; she would have to hurry. She was meeting her attorney, David Skinner. He would be in the park, across from the sheriff's office at ten o'clock, near the left entrance by the gazebo.

By the time she reached the park, LaRae was running; the navy and white shoulder bag bounced painfully against her hip until she was sure it would leave a bruise. She spotted him standing at the entrance of the gazebo where he said he would be, looking charming as always for a mature gentleman.

He wore a medium gray suite with a blue shirt underneath topped with a tie, which picked up the colors of the suit and the shirt in it. His thick dark brown hair held just enough graying around the temples to look distinguishing.

LaRae sat down beside him, holding her purse in her lap while she gasped for breath. "Made it," she panted, waiting for her pulse rate to return to normal before she said another word.

"Now, remember you don't sign any paperwork without me going over it first and then giving you the okay. You understand?"

"Yes." LaRae shook her head to emphasis her agreement.

"Are you ready to face Goliath?"

LaRae stood, brushed the front of the navy blue and white pants suite she wore, pasted on a fake half smile, and then fell in step beside David Skinner. After crossing the street directly in front of the sheriff's office, LaRae and David entered the building, taking the stairs to the second floor, as instructed by Sheriff Blanks; the two opened the door, exactly on time, to the room where the meeting was to be held.

"LaRae...David...glad to see you." Jason greeted. After shaking hands he then directed them to two chairs across from two mature, well-dressed gentlemen seated at a long table.

"Hello Jason." David greeted while guiding LaRae to her seat.

"Hello Jason. Hello Mr. Garth." LaRae greeted before taking her seat across from the gentlemen all ready seated at the table.

"Gentlemen this is LaRae Jones and her attorney David Skinner."

LaRae noticed immediately, the worried look on both attorneys' face when David was introduced as her attorney. "These gentlemen are attorneys Steven Goldberg and Henry Johnson." Jason made the introductions.

"Ms. Jones you had no need...of legal representation...we...we just had some minor...paperwork for you to sign...that's all." Henry Johnson faintly stammered.

Henry, though the taller and much slimmer of the two gentlemen had thinning gray hair with a receding hairline. From his appearance she bet he considered himself the more debonair of the two. Steven Goldberg, on the other hand, was just the opposite of Henry Johnson. He had a head full of thick curly white hair, LaRae noticed. Though the suite he wore looked nice and fit him well, it had not been specially tailored to fit every curve and inch of his body as Mr. Johnson's had. Right up front she could tell Mr. Henry Johnson, through his meticulous dress, was a man that wanted others to view him as a person of elegance and importance.

"Gentlemen, may we have a look at that paperwork you were talking about?" David directed his question to Henry Johnson since he took the lead in the meeting.

"Sure, it's right here." Henry shuffled through his briefcase for a few seconds before pulling out several sheets of legal papers and placing them in front of LaRae. Keeping his hand on the papers, he flipped them to the last sheet and then handed her a pen. "I just need you to sign right here above your name and we'll be through here."

LaRae pushed his hand off the papers, picked them up off the table, and handed them to David. "I will after my attorney looks them over and says its okay." She calmly replied.

After briefly reading through some of the papers David looked across the table at the men then spoke, "Excuse me; according to these papers you want Ms. Jones to sign she would be relinquishing all claims left in the will back to Ashcroft Enterprise." David Skinner looked Henry Johnson directly in the face and asked. "What claims?" Henry Johnson worriedly looked to Steven Goldberg for answers.

"Do you have a copy of the will with you?"

Henry once more shuffled around in his briefcase then looked toward Steven. "Do you have a copy with you, Steven?"

David could tell these attorneys didn't want his client or him to see her ex-husband's will. He removed one of his business cards and tossed it across the table to Henry Johnson.

"I'll tell you what—here's my card when you get back to Boston mail a copy of the will to my office. I'll keep these papers you wanted my client to blindly sign and if everything turns out to be kosher after reading the will, then my client will sign them and I'll get them back to you." He tapped LaRae on the shoulder. "Let's go, I believe we're finished here."

LaRae stood and turned to the gentlemen still seated at the table. "Good day gentlemen." She then turned toward Jason and Gilbert Garth. "Good bye Mr. Garth, will we be seeing more of you this time before you have to leave town?"

"The Sheriff has invited me for supper tonight at his Aunt's."

"Wonderful. Good bye Jason."

"Good bye LaRae." Jason then addressed the gentlemen who were now in irritated whispered conversation at the table. "Gentlemen I believe your meeting has concluded, and since it has I need my conference room back." The gentlemen quickly gathered their paperwork, closed their briefcases, and left the room.

LaRae, as she did often, had joined the group and their guest, Gilbert Garth, for supper; they were gathered in the parlor for the traditional evening coffee and conversation when the front door bell was heard ringing.

"Who could that be at this late hour?" Shirley wondered aloud.

"I'll go see." Jason volunteered.

Soon the group heard Jason and another male voice in conversation as they advanced down the hallway toward the parlor.

"Come on in, She's in here with the rest of the guest." Jason entered the room followed by David Skinner. "I think everybody knows David. David you met Gilbert at my office this morning."

"Yes, I did. Hello Mr. Garth." David walked over and shook Gilbert's hand.

"It's Gilbert and hello again."

"David would you like coffee." Shirley asked as she rose from her chair to hug his neck.

"Yes, please...just black," David said with eagerness in his voice.

LaRae with a questionable look upon her face finally asked. "David what are you doing here at this hour? Are you looking for me?"

"Well, yes, I am." And, wasting no time and accepting the cup of coffee from Shirley, he walked over and pulled up a chair beside LaRae before continuing the conversation. "The two big city attorneys we met with this morning called me and wanted to set up a meeting; I just left them about an hour ago. I've been looking for you every since meeting with them. It seems they could come up with a copy of your ex-husband's will after all."

LaRae astonished just looked at him at first unable to speak. "And...and...what did they say...did it say?"

"I can tell you one thing they come to town thinking they were dealing with a little country bumpkin of a girl." David started laughing. "I'm so glad you called me to represent you. It was worth it to see the look on their faces when you walked in with your own attorney."

"Yes, it was." Jason and Gilbert both chimed in at the same time.

LaRae's impatience starting to show, asked again. "What did you find out?"

"Well, young lady I found out you're not going to have to worry about money for some time now, if ever. Besides a large amount of money your ex-husband listed certain items of jewelry, antiques, an automobile, artwork, and real-estate property that you were to inherit upon his death."

"What? How can that be? We were divorced."

"He never took you out of his will. You were his soul heir. But that's not the kicker—the main thing that had them worried and all in a tizzy—that they tried to cheat you out of besides the money and other items listed—was your ex-husband left you the controlling shares of Ashcroft Enterprise. *You* own fifty-five percent of the shares—fifty-five percent of Ashcroft Enterprise."

"You have got to be kidding me." LaRae was astounded at this news.

David looked at her before proclaiming. "They want to buy you out."

"After the stunt they pulled today, I'm sure it's going to be a fair price." LaRae's sarcasm escaped before she could stop it.

David waited a few minutes to let everything he had just told her sink in before speaking again, "As your attorney, my advice to you would be to wait, hold on to your shares, and let me check out the company before you do anything."

"That sounds like sound advice to me; except I would add one more important element to it, pray before doing anything." Shirley told her.

"I agree with Shirley. You shouldn't decide an important decision like this without first praying." Mr. Potts added.

LaRae looked at her attorney and told him. "I agree; David you can meet with the gentlemen tomorrow and tell them my decision."

He smiled at her sensible decision then told her. "I'll be glad to inform them." He rose to leave and remembered the check in the pocket of his jacket, he reached his hand into the front of his jacket and removed a folded piece of paper and handed it to her. "Oh, I almost forgot, this is for you."

LaRae unfolded the paper and looked at it. "Oh, my—oh, my—is this for real," she gasped. She was astounded when she read the amount on the check, two hundred and fifty thousand dollars. She had never seen so much money at one time. She knew nothing about James' company; though he spent extravagantly on himself, he was always frugal when it came to spending money on her. The most money he ever gave her at one time was fifty dollars. As for herself, she always had to watch her spending to make sure to keep enough cash on hand incase of having to pack and run at a minutes notice, often in the middle of the night.

"Oh, yes, it's for real and the attorneys said it was the first; you would be receiving others like it every quarter for five years. It has nothing to do with the shares; it's a separate settlement. I made arrangements for the checks to be sent in care of my office, I didn't think they needed your home address." He looked to her for acknowledgement of the arrangement he made with the other attorneys. After receiving a nod of the head from her, he continued, "At this meeting I'll also make arrangements with them on all the items listed in the will—you are suppose to inherit—being delivered to my office if that's alright with you."

"That's fine, thank you David for looking out for me." She rose and hugged him goodbye.

Arriving home, LaRae, needing answers, went straight to her prayer closet. It was a small, downstairs room across from a bigger bedroom, which appeared as if it could have been a nursery at one time. She chose it to fix up for her prayer room. She prayed late into the night and early morning before she felt a release; yet, she still felt she had no answers to her unbearable past.

After a quick breakfast of oatmeal, toast, orange juice, and coffee, LaRae made herself stay busy until every last box and container was emptied and the items within put away in a proper place. She worked through the morning.

Realizing the noon hour had passed, she fixed a light lunch consisting of a tuna salad sandwich, a few cucumber spears with sliced tomatoes seasoned to taste and a glass of tea. Placing her meal on a tray she carried it to the terrace to enjoy the view along with the cool breeze. Although her meal was completed, LaRae continued to linger on the terrace and take-in the splendor of her surroundings.

"Father, What a wonderful place you have given to me. It has got to be a little piece of heaven here on earth. There's nothing I've seen to match it. The beauty of the view, the gentleness of the wildlife, even the tranquility of the surroundings is beyond comparison. Thank you."

After placing her dirty dishes in the sink, she gathered all the empty boxes and plastic containers together and carried them to the attic. Noticing all the dust and spider webs, she retrieved cleaning supplies from the utility room and made her way back to the attic. By the time she reached the halfway point, LaRae was running out of steam, her shoulders and legs ached until she was sure she would be sore by tomorrow morning. She looked at her watch; it read eight o'clock. After a lingering hot bath, LaRae crept straight away into bed.

Slow to rise the next morning she put off completing the cleaning in the attic until after lunch. Then, with cleaning supplies in hand once more she climbed the stairs to the attic. Dusting and sweeping as she went, she made her way around the room to the distant corner from the stairway. She had been saving this area for last, knowing it would take the most work. Because in this corner some old board had been scattered and piled, over waist high to her and about as wide, against the back wall. She slowly begins to neatly stack the boards a little distance away.

After several hours of pulling, carrying, and stacking, boards, LaRae noticed the top of an old trunk in the middle of the pile of old, scattered boards. Eager to get to it, she quickened the pace of removing the boards heaped around and about the trunk.

"You had better be worth all the sore muscles I'll have tomorrow." She said after finally freeing the trunk from the last of the old boards. Pulling the old trunk over in front of the west windows, she eased down and sits on the floor before it. She carefully loosened the old leather straps and the brass latches; then she very slowly opened the lid— overwhelmed with anticipation at peeking inside—yet, afraid of being disappointed.

Disappointed, she was not. The trunk was stuffed full of old treasures. She came to that conclusion after only quickly looking through the items in the top drawer. It only took a few minutes of shuffling through several items on this shelf to know the trunk belong to her late Great Aunt Kate.

LaRae gently picked up several lace trimmed linen handkerchiefs, which were hand embroidered with tiny delicate flowers, birds, and butterflies. There were three pieces of finely crafted jewelry labeled with pieces of paper now yellowed and slightly dried with age. Picking up each piece, careful not to disturb the old worn labels, LaRae read each. The first she picked up was a beautiful, petite, gold wedding set, which had belonged to LaRae's Great Grandmother Sarah, Sarah Katharine Woods. It had an emerald for a center stone, which was surrounded by diamonds. The second piece she picked up was another wedding set, which had belonged to Great Aunt Kate, Mary Katharine Kent. It had a diamond in the center flanked by a diamond on each side. The last piece she removed from the trunk was a delicate gold filigree cross, which hung from a dainty gold chain. This too had belonged to Aunt Kate. Upon closer inspection LaRae noted the chain was broken. "I'll see if I can get this fixed. It's so beautiful." She said as she placed the elegant piece back on the shelf beside the other jewelry.

She continued to rummage through the items in the top drawer, finding a soft leather beige pouch, which when unrolled contained different sizes of crochet, tatting, and knitting needles. Beside the leather pouch were located some embroidery hoops tied together with two blue ribbons. Also there were several carefully wrapped small magnificent different colored glass vases and bowls, along with some unique pieces of etched crystal. The last thing she picked up was Aunt Kate's black leather bound Bible. With great care she opened the pages soon coming across a page where Aunt Kate had written the names of each family member with the dates of birth, marriage and death printed out beside each name.

Gently replacing each item, except for the Bible, LaRae carefully removed the top drawer from the trunk so she could see what new surprises were hiding beneath. Placed on the top was an elegant, flowing Antebellum-style wedding gown, white with baby blue embroidered trimming on the bodice and down each sleeve. A great many of hours of hard work went into the making of this dress she thought, letting her hand run over the soft material of the gown. Underneath the dress she found the complete wedding attire with matching transparent veil. Examining each piece, she could tell they were handmade.

Placing the wedding ensemble to the side, she noticed four medium sized packages also wrapped and worn with aged paper just as all the other items in the trunk. After unwrapping each packet, inside she found tiny hand made baby clothing. She fingered each little gown, bunting, sweater, cap, and booties. Under these were six finely crocheted blankets. Holding the baby garments in her hands, LaRae wondered. She knew Aunt Kate had no living children of her own. These items had to mean she was pregnant and either lost the child before or during birth; or she lost it during infancy.

The next thing to catch her attention was a set of eight leather bound books placed neatly under the baby clothing. Picking one up and gently flipping through the pages, it didn't take long to realize these books were a set of journals kept by her Aunt Kate. With the sun starting to set and the light growing dim in the attic, LaRae gathered together the journals and set them aside as she replaced most of the items back in the old trunk.

Grabbing Her Aunt Kate's Bible and journals she headed downstairs for the night, promising herself she would finish searching out the trunk later. Placing the Bible in her prayer room she then took the journals upstairs to her bedroom. Putting them on her bedside table for easy access on the nights when she couldn't sleep, she showered, then dawning a nightgown and robe, returned downstairs to fix a light meal for the night.

After preparing herself for bed, she removed the journals from the bedside table and arranged them by dates in which they were written, from earliest dates backwards. Taking the book on top of the stack and placing it on the top of the bedside table, she then places the remaining books on a shelf under the table.

Propping pillows against the headboard of the bed and leaning comfortably back, LaRae got ready for an excursion into Aunt Kate's life. The first few pages told of events and arrangements leading up to the wedding ceremony between Aunt Kate and Uncle Joe. The wedding attire upstairs in the attic was Great Grandmother Sarah's prior to Aunt Kate's. She wrote of her joy of being able to wear her mother's dress and of the slight alteration that had to be made to it. LaRae laid the book against her chest and closed her eyes picturing the excitement around Great Grandfather Frank's house with the preparations for the wedding of his oldest daughter.

April 10th
The day before my wedding. Mamma and Papa came to my room last night and gave me a beautiful gold filigree cross necklace. As Papa was putting the necklace around my neck, Mamma told me to remember how I was raised, knowing God, and when times get tough to clasp the cross tight in my hand to remember God never leaves me or forsakes me. He would walk me through the darkest hours. I thanked them and then I was sad that I would be moving so far away from my family.

After reading through to where Uncle Joe brought his young bride back to Arkansas, LaRae placed a marker between the pages and closed the book. Placing the journal on the table beside the bed, she turned off the lamp.

The next morning LaRae awoke late. Skipping breakfast, she quickly dresses in a pale blue summer suite with white sandals. Twisting her long hair in a bun high on the back of her head, she hurried out the back door to the garage. She maneuvered her car down the long driveway and increased her speed once she was on the road headed toward town. LaRae pulled into an empty space in the Believers Church parking lot just as her friends were exiting their vehicle. Quickening her steps, she walked into the building with the group taking her usual seat between Shirley and Jason.

Pastor Jenkins opened the service with announcements of upcoming events then went straight into hymns of praise. No longer caring how her voice sounded to others immediately around her, LaRae let the words of praise to her Lord come forth from her mouth. As always with Bible in hand, she listened eagerly as the minister started his sermon.

His message was on forgiveness. She listened as he told the congregation, "I know this one is a hard one for some of you but you need to forgive those whom have hurt and persecuted you. You're not forgiving them for their sake but for your own. Do you remember when Evangelist Paul Toby visited our church a few Sundays back? He ministered to you on healing. Healing and forgiveness go hand in hand. You cannot hold unforgiveness in your heart against someone.

"God tells us in His word we have to forgive." Malachi Jenkins paused and opened his Bible before reading, "For if you forgive men their trespasses, your heavenly Father will also forgive you but if ye forgive not men their trespasses, neither will your Father forgive your trespasses." LaRae watched as he turned more pages in his Bible and begins ministering once more. "Mark Chapter Eleven tells us 'and when you stand praying, forgive, if you have ought against any: that your Father also which is in heaven may forgive you your trespasses But if you do not forgive, neither will your Father which is in heaven forgive your trespasses'." She felt the Lord was speaking directly to her with each word Pastor Jenkins spoke. She knew she had to forgive James for all the horrible things he put her through, but when she thinks she's accomplished it; an anger builds deep inside of her, at just the mention of his name.

She dabbed at the tear gathering in her eyes as she exited the sanctuary. Following Shirley's car with Jason in the driver's seat back to the *Country Living Bed & Breakfast*, she thought on the pastor's message especially the scripture verses he used. LaRae begins to pray, "Father I know I have to forgive James for all the wrong he did to me, all the fear and humiliation he put me through. Father you know all the pain I suffered from his hands." She paused to wipe the tears, which were flowing freely down her cheeks. "Father I can't do it— I just can't do it—right now, I have nothing but anger and hate inside of me for this man—who took so much from me! I'm sorry. I'm trying." She stopped praying, wiped her face, and pulled her car into the driveway beside Shirley's.

With the noon meal complete the small group retreated to the parlor. Although tourist season was at hand and the *Bed & Breakfast* was booked to capacity; this room was reserved for Shirley's personal family and friends.

Shirley noting the redden eyes and the troubled look upon LaRae's face throughout the noon meal finally asked, "What's bothering you Baby Doll?"

"I don't know if I can do it." LaRae hopelessly responded.

"Do what?"

"Forgive—like Pastor Jenkins said in his message this morning— we have to." She looked up at Shirley with tears in her eyes. "I know I have to, and I want to, but I don't know if I can."

"It will come. Give it time." Shirley knew immediately who LaRae was having trouble forgiving. "Keep praying and asking for God's help to forgive him, because you will never be able to do it on your own."

"But you don't understand, I—I—I hate him!" She was ashamed to admit such feeling to her friends.

"I understand completely those feelings. When Jason's parents, my sister Alice and her husband Robert, were killed in an accident by a drunk driver, who walked away with only a broken arm; I was angry. I hated the drunk driver that killed them." She stopped and looked at LaRae. "I had to pray through the anger and hate to be able to get to forgiveness."

"But what do I pray?"

"There's no set prayer, Baby Doll, you have to pray what's in your heart. Just be honest with God, because He already knows what you hold deep inside you. He knows how you feel and the desires of your heart."

"And His Word says He will give you the desires of your heart," Professor Cove added to the conversation.

Mr. Potts stood up and pulled a small black box from his jacket pocket and walked over to stand in front of LaRae. "I'd like to give this to you. It belonged to my wife, Margaret." He opened the box and removed a thick gold chain bracelet with one charm dangling from it; he then held it to where he could read the inscription written across the charm, "*I will never leave thee nor forsake thee Hebrews 13:5.*"

"It's beautiful, but are you sure."

"I think she would be pleased to have it pass own to you. I believe it helped her walk through some of her darkest hours. It was given to her by her parents as a wedding gift just before she married her first husband." LaRae looked at him curiously. "My wife went through some bad things at the hands of her first husband before he died. She too had to forgive before passing on to be with the Lord." LaRae held her right arm out in front of Mr. Potts and he fastened the bracelet around it.

Night had fallen upon the small town by the time LaRae backed her car out of the driveway of the *Bed & Breakfast* and headed toward her own home. Dropping her purse and keys on the entryway table and walking straight through to the terrace, she eased down into a chair. Thinking over and over on the message Pastor Jenkins preached in today's service, she once more begin to pray, "Father I know I have to forgive James—I don't like having all this bitterness and hate for him in my heart—but I just can't do it by myself—all the pain is still too fresh—I need your help." She fingered the charm hanging loosely from the bracelet Mr. Potts had just given her earlier. "Father walk with me through these trying times. Plant the seed of forgiveness in my heart that I might forgive, because, right now I can't find any forgiveness in me." The tears flowed freely down her cheeks continuously until the well run dry. She then reentered the house, walked up the stairs to her bedroom, readied herself for bed, and then collapsed into bed from emotional exhaustion.

Unable to return to the reading of Aunt Kate's journal until three days later, LaRae grabs it off of the bedside table, fixes a glass of tea, and retires to the terrace, soon after completing her morning chores. Opening the book to the marker she placed between the pages a few days ago, she read were upon arriving in Arkansas Uncle Joe and Aunt Kate moves into the Kent family home with Uncle Joe's parents; then how at Uncle Joe request, Aunt Kate learns from Mrs. Kent her way of cooking and doing household chores. She continued reading into the month of August two years later where Mr. Kent, Uncle Joe and his older brother, Henry started building on a smaller home for the parents; where in turn Uncle Joe and Aunt Kate would inherit the larger home, since Henry and his wife already had a nice home.

LaRae, looking at her watch, noticed she had been so engrossed in the journal she missed her noon meal and evening was upon her. Placing the book on the table she walked to the kitchen and fixed a meal consisting of a small baked chicken breast, salad, a baked potato, and a glass of milk. Putting the food on a tray she walked back out to the terrace to enjoy her meal. Completing the meal she continued to linger at the table taking pleasure in the cool breeze gently blowing across the terrace, and the view of the wonderful sunset spread out before her. Stacking the dishes on the tray and picking up the journal, LaRae entered the house for the night, locking the door behind her.

Every evening LaRae read on Aunt Kate's journals. By the time she read a few pages into the fourth book, LaRae noted a change in Aunt Kate's handwriting. Instead of her usual even flowing beautiful script, it had become more scribbled and hard to read; the tone of the journal had changed too, it seemed sadder, more aloft for some reason. Reading a few more pages, she soon found out why the handwriting and tone of the journals changed.

June 12th

Joe came home in the middle of the day, madder than a skunk, don't know what set him off; can't blame it on the demon, alcohol, this time because he hadn't had a drop, like before. He just started cursing, hitting, and demanding something to eat. When I tried to tell him his lunch wasn't ready yet; he became even more violent throwing me around the room, slapping me across the face. I don't know what happened to set him off. I'm always so careful to watch what I do and say so as not to anger him, because I know he has such a temper. I wish Mom and Pop Kent had never moved out, because she always seemed to know how to handle him when he gets this way.

June 20th

Joe has put a lock on the outside of the attic door and has taken to locking me inside while he is away from the house. He has been gone for four days now. Yet, I don't mind. It's sad when I prefer the silence of the attic to the company of my own husband. But he has changed so much from the charming gentleman I met back home. When we first met I could do no wrong, now everything I do is wrong. It seems now I can do no right.

June 24th
The attic has become my permanent room. He has moved a bed and some of my belongings up here. I'm allowed out to cook and do daily chores; the rest of the time I spend locked up here in the attic.

She, slowly placing the marker between the pages of the book, closed it and placed it on the nightstand beside the bed. Horror at what she'd read that day still resounding in her head.

Awaking early from a restless night's sleep, LaRae slowly got out of bed and headed downstairs to the kitchen. Having only coffee for breakfast, she went back upstairs to shower and dress for the day. Avoiding even a glance toward the stairway leading to the attic, she quickly walked through the house exiting out the back door. With cane in hand she walked the property, slow at first, then her pace quickened. Though her knee ached, she continued walking, like a driving force within her kept urging her forward. She walked, and walked.

Looking at her watch, LaRae realized she had been walking for a long time and distance. According to her watch, the time was three o'clock in the afternoon. Turning around and looking in the direction of the house to get her bearings, she calculated the shortest distance would be cutting across a farmer's already cut and baled hayfield; since it butted up against the boundaries of her own property. Crossing the hayfield, she came upon a small creek, which was the dividing line between the two properties; just as she crossed the creek her attention was drawn toward two small headstones underneath a large maple tree. Bewildered at finding graves on her property, she walked up to the headstones and wiped the dirt from the front of them in hopes of reading the names. On the one closer to her she read, "Baby boy Kent." On the next stone she read, "Baby Kent." There were no names, no birth dates, nothing, except for what she had just read. Puzzled over the situation, she continued on through the wooded area of her own land back to her home.

After two weeks, unable to stay away from the journals any longer, LaRae picked the one up off the bedside table, which held the marker between its pages, and began to read.

September 6ᵗʰ
I'm not being kept locked in the attic any more, every since last month when Mom Kent dropped in for an unexpected visit to find me locked in. I lied and said I was cleaning and the wind must of had blown the door closed. I know she didn't believe me.
I believe I'm in the family way. Every morning for over a week I've woken up sick. I'm so excited. I'm going to have a baby. I don't know how Joe will feel. I'll tell the family in a couple of weeks when I know for sure. Mom and Pop Kent are continuously asking when we are going to give them grandchildren.

September 20ᵗʰ
Tonight at a family dinner over at Mom and Pop Kent's house I announced that Joe and I were going to have a baby. Joe appeared happy over the fact we were having a baby. He treated me real kind. He was the charming man he used to be when I first met him. I hope this baby is a boy and we can name it after Joe and his paw.

October 3ʳᵈ
Joe beat me viciously again last night; I don't understand what's gotten into him; his attitude about the baby changed. The more joy his parents showed toward this baby and the more attention I received from them, the angrier he got. He continued to hit me over and over in the stomach, holding me by my long braid so I could not run away from him; I kept covering up to protect the baby. He then flung me down the stairs.

October 17ᵗʰ
I lost the baby two days after Joe threw me down the stairs. He told his parents I slipped and had a bad fall down the stairs. Pop Kent came to me when Joe wasn't around and told me he buried my baby under the big maple beside the creek beyond the woods. I didn't understand why things were done that way and I didn't ask. Mom Kent has made it a point to stay here at our house since I lost the baby. Her being here has caused Joe to be on his best behavior.

LaRae finished reading the third book; it was more of the same. Uncle Joe's abuse of Aunt Kate started again soon after his mother moved back to her own home and her frequent visits to their home slacked off. LaRae placed the journal on the shelf under the bedside table, turned off the lamp and tried to sleep.

Once more for days, she could not pick up another journal and read it. The books were full of so much pain and heartache it was all she could do to keep from crying. After knowing the attic stairway lead to her aunt's prison, she had to look in the opposite direction every time she walked up the stairs to enter her bedroom.

Finally after a week and a half, LaRae felt a necessity within her to finish the journals. She walked up the stairs, picked up the unread books, marched up the stairs to the attic, opened the door, found a comfortable seat, and sat down to read.

The fifth book read like the others with one exception, she had received word of her mother's death. Of course she was not allowed to attend the funeral. Many beatings were handed out for the littlest mistake, sometimes she never knew what she was being beaten for. She was once more a prisoner in the attic. Yet to her the attic had become her sanctuary, as long as she was up in the attic Uncle Joe didn't exist.

In the sixth book Uncle Joe's brother, Henry, died in a logging accident. She continued to be held in the attic and the abuse never stops. Yet, he would never enter the attic; he would bring her down stairs to abuse her or make her perform her wifely duties them throw her back into the attic. LaRae continued though the words were heartbreaking to read. She had almost finished the book when she read were Aunt Kate believed she was pregnant again and how she was trying hard to hide it from Uncle Joe.

She opened the seventh book and begins to read. Even though a night sky had long fallen over the town LaRae remained in the attic with Aunt Kate's journals determined to complete them. She reads where Uncle Joe finds out about the pregnancy and is excited about the upcoming birth as is his family. Uncle Joe, as with the other pregnancy, begins to treat her kinder. His mother begins to visit more often and she and Aunt Kate sew baby cloths. Then something happens, Aunt Kate tells how Uncle Joe starts staying away from home for days at a time, coming home drunk, or yelling and cursing at her when his mother isn't around.

Then the words jump off the page at LaRae, running through her mind, digging up memories. Tears flowed down her cheeks as she read the next entry.

March 14th
Joe came home drunk and on a rampage again. Beating me severely I tried to run away but being seven months pregnant I only made it to the front yard. He threw me down on the hard ground kicking and stomping my stomach, and kept yelling, "I'll stomp that baby out of you—you fat pig," over and over. I lost him that night. I know my baby was a boy because Pop Kent told me when he told me he buried my little boy beside my other baby. Pop Kent also told me he had sent word to my sister, Lois, and she was coming for another visit. I'm glad Lois is coming even though Joe doesn't like her being here.

The tears continued to flow freely from LaRae's eyes, a memory she didn't want to visit now so fresh, as if it happened yesterday. Her one and only pregnancy ended by James, just as Uncle Joe ended Aunt Kate's. All because she was pregnant and couldn't fit into an expensive sleek dress he had bought her. She remembers his words to this day when she reminded him she was pregnant. "*I can take care of that little problem.*" He told her and begins to beat her and throws her to the ground, where he kicks and stomps until she lost the baby that night. But that wasn't enough for James Ashcroft, who wanted to make sure nothing ever happened like that again. Contacting a personal friend who was also a surgeon, and making arrangements for a hysterectomy to be done against her wishes, and not once did anyone ever listen to her protests. So not only did James take her only baby from that pregnancy away; but also made sure she could never have a chance for any more. *My baby was a little problem to him—a little problem.*

LaRae was emotionally spent by the time she finished reading the seventh journal. She walked over to the bed that she now knew had been Aunt Kate's, kicked off her shoes, lay on the bed and pulled a blanket over her and hoped for some sleep.

Arising early the next morning from a surprisingly peaceful sleep, she picked up the eighth and final journal walked downstairs to her bedroom to shower and change her cloths. After eating a light breakfast LaRae walked out to the terrace with book in hand to complete the reading of it.

Opening the book she starts to read, only a few pages in she finds out Uncle Joe had been killed in a fight with another man. The man pleaded self-defense and was never charged. Aunt Kate, dawned mourning clothes, watched as the man, who had reined terror for many years over her life, was lowered six feet into the ground. Then upon returning home, not knowing what to do with herself, she sunk into a depression. LaRae also read of how everyone around believed the depression was because of Aunt Kate missing Uncle Joe so very much; reading on she saw how the concerned neighbor's very words snapped Aunt Kate out of her depression.

Feeling slight hunger pains growling, LaRae looked at her watch and noted the time was well past the noon hour; laying the journal aside she eased out of the chair and entered the kitchen and fixed herself a light lunch. Restraining herself from picking back up the book, until she had completed the meal she'd prepared and then tided up the kitchen; she once more immersed herself in the journal.

May 17th
I have just emerged from my prayer closet after twenty-one days of prayer and fasting for God to help me forgive Joe of all the horrible and painful things he put me through. Peace has come at last. I'll never forget the things he has done to me but I am now able to forgive him and move forward. My Lord, My Savior, has applied His healing balm to all the open wounds Joe caused and soon very soon they will only be scars. I will remember how I got the scars but they will no longer hurt. They will only be scars, healed opened bleeding wounds. I also know now what God will have me do until He calls me home. He wants me to use this house, which saw so much suffering and abuse, and make it a safe haven, a sanctuary, for other women who are suffering as I myself suffered.

LaRae read how Aunt Kate employed different tactic to rescue women and if these women had children the children too, whom were being abused by their husbands. After the death of Pop Kent, Mom Kent soon joined forces with Aunt Kate in helping liberate women from their abusers. "Aunt Kate and Mom Kent built an underground railroad for abused women way back then," speaking respectfully of her kin-people. In the closing pages of the last journal Aunt Kate mentioned having had a vision that led to her decision to leave the house and property to LaRae, but she never said anymore about it.

By the time LaRae completed the book the time was way into the night hour, but she continued to sit on the terrace marveling over all she had read. Her own Grandmother Lois had joined troops with Aunt Kate and Mom Kent. The more LaRae thought about it she remembered some of the women that were, *just hitching a ride*, with us back to Louisiana. She had found a list of names of all the women that had passed through this house to somewhere else for a saver life. Aunt Kate had helped many, many women. Now LaRae knew what she had to do, entering her prayer room and closing the door behind her, she fell upon her knees before the alter.

CHAPTER 11

LaRae emerged from her prayer room forty days later, walked upstairs to her bedroom; showered, put on a nightgown, and then laid across her bed pulling the blanket up around her. She had spent the last forty days and night nights fasting and praying, pouring her heart out to God, for direction and answers from Him; during this time she consumed only water. She awoke to the site of her friend, Shirley, sitting in the rocking chair across the room, softly singing her favorite hymn and slowly rocking back and forth crocheting on something she held in her hands.

"How long have I been asleep?"

"Just about a day."

"How long have you been babysitting?"

"Every since you fell asleep, I knew this was your first time to fast. I wanted to make sure you were okay." LaRae gave Shirley a curious look, not understanding all of what she was talking about. "I call fasting my sacrificial prayer; because when I need to hear from God so desperately I'm willing to sacrifice something, which is usually food, until I do." LaRae nodded her head in understanding. At first she didn't know that fasting was what she was doing. She only knew she needed to hear from God—she needed direction from Him—to know for sure what her next step would be, concerning what to do with her own life and the house Aunt Kate had left her.

"Are you hungry?"

LaRae thought for a minute, "no not really." She replied.

"There must still be something the Lord wants to do before you're released from your fast." Shirley walked to the door. "I'll wait for you downstairs with the others."

"Others…?"

"Yes, we have all been here for you off and on praying with you, either as a group or one at a time, you have never been alone."

LaRae climbed out of bed and dressed in pale blue Capri pants with a white knit pullover top with contrasting needle work stitching, which matched the pants. After pulling her long blond hair high in a bun on her head, she left the room and headed downstairs to be with her friends, who had always been there for her no matter what she'd been through.

Entering the kitchen, she noticed Pastor Jenkins and his wife were also sitting around the table with her other friends.

"Good morning…I mean afternoon Pastor Jenkins and Sister Ella, Mr. Potts, Professor, and Jason." She greeted, with embracement, for still being in the bed, showing on her face. Taking the glass of water Shirley offered she turned, thanked her, and then seated herself at the table next to Pastor Jenkins.

Pastor Jenkins looked at LaRae then started speaking. The Lord sent me here to speak to you about the baptism in the Holy Ghost. LaRae never interrupted; she just listened to what her minister was saying. Pastor Jenkins pulled out his Bible and opened it to *The Acts of the Apostles* chapter one and told her to read aloud verses four and five, which were highlighted in yellow in his Bible.

LaRae, as she began to read, noticed most of the words were in red which meant Jesus himself was speaking, "*And, being assembled together with them, commanded them that they should not depart from Jerusalem, but wait for the promise of the Father, which, saith he, ye have heard of me. For John truly baptized with water; but ye shall be baptized with the Holy Ghost not many days hence.*"

"Now drop down and read verse eight in the same chapter."

LaRae scanned with her finger down the page stopping it at verse eight and started to read. *"But ye shall receive power, after that the Holy Ghost is come upon you: and ye shall be witnesses unto me both in Jerusalem, and in all Judea, and in Samaria, and unto the uttermost part of the earth."*

Pastor Jenkins took the Bible back from LaRae and flipped back a few pages to the book of *St. John* chapter fourteen. He laid it on the table where LaRae could read along with him, and pointed to verse twenty-six as he read aloud. *"But the Comforter, which is the Holy Ghost, whom the Father will send in my name, he shall teach you all things, and bring all things to your remembrance, whatsoever I have said unto you."* Pastor Jenkins continuing in the same book showed her other verses in chapters fifteen and sixteen where Jesus talked about the Comforter. He then flipped the pages back to the book of *the Acts of the Apostles* and had her read first, she read from chapter two verses one through four.

"And when the day of Pentecost was fully come, they were all with one accord in one place. And suddenly there came a sound from heaven as of a rushing mighty wind, and it filled all the house where they were sitting. ³And there appeared unto them cloven tongues like as of fire and it sat upon each of them. And they were all filled with the Holy Ghost, and began to speak with other tongues, as the Spirit gave them utterance."

Pastor Jenkins then turned a few pages over to chapter eight in the same book and explained to her, "The apostles were gathered in Jerusalem and heard that Samaria had received the word of God so they sent John and Peter to Samaria. Now you pick up with verse fifteen and read through seventeen."

LaRae started to read, *"who, when they were come down, prayed for them, that they might receive the Holy Ghost: (For as yet He was fallen upon none of them: only they were baptized into the name of the Lord Jesus.) Then laid they their hands on them, and they received the Holy Ghost."* Pastor Jenkins, also, showed her other scripture about receiving the Holy Ghost.

He then turned to her and asked, "Do you understand what you have just read or do I need to explain it more to you?"

"No, I understand all the scriptures I have read." Now understanding why the Lord had sent Pastor Jenkins and his wife to her.

Pastor Jenkins and all of the group stood to their feet and moved to stand behind him. "Then stand and receive the baptism in the Holy Ghost." LaRae stood to her feet and the group formed a circle around her as Malachi Jenkins laid his hands upon her head and said, "Receive ye now the Holy Ghost and fire." LaRae's whole body trembled as she was filled with the Holy Ghost, and began to speak with other tongues as the Spirit gave her utterance. She began to speak the Word of God with boldness and authority. The small group was amazed by it; because they knew how shy she usually was. She ministered as a mature Christian instead of a new baby just a few months old.

"I'm famished." LaRae announced after the Spirit had lifted. "I'm in the mood for grilled hamburgers this evening and it's no fun to grill alone. Do y'all want to join me on the terrace?"

"We'll stay and eat with you." Shirley announced. "But did you forget that you just came off of a forty day fast, Baby Doll?" LaRae just looked at her. "You have to reintroduce food slowly back into your system."

Shirley prepared a very small piece of salmon seasoned to taste, wrapped it in foil, and then placed it on the platter with the hamburger meat for the men to grill.

While LaRae prepared a potato salad, she made a cream of potato soup then the three women gathered the condiments, bread and serving utensils which were placed on a tray and carried out to the terrace. The men were already at work at the grill when the ladies stepped out on the terrace. Taking a seat beside Shirley, LaRae scanned the small group she had known a short time, by most people's standards, yet, she had become so comfortable with them, as if she had always known them. "Mmm, it all smells so good" LaRae said sniffing the aroma of the juicy meat.

Malachi Jenkins flipped the patties once more to be sure they had cooked sufficiently before he turned off the grill. Stacking the patties and the small foil wrapped package on a plate, he passed it to Jason, who in turn passed it toward the table; then turning back to the grill Pastor Jenkins gathered the roasted corn on the cob on to another plate and passed it to Jason. With all the food on the table the group gathered around the table and LaRae asked Pastor Jenkins to ask grace.

The next morning LaRae awoke feeling refreshed, renewed and with a song in her spirit. She showered, dressed for the day, and descended the stairs headed for the kitchen, singing Shirley's favorite hymn. After completing a very light breakfast, she went straight to her office, where she sat down at the large desk, situated in front of three large windows. She then pulled out stationary, and started in on writing two long overdue letters. Completing the letters, addressing each, and then placing the correct postage on each she walked down to the end of the driveway and placed them in the mailbox.

With Sunday service over and gathered in Shirley's parlor with her friends, LaRae made her announcement.

"I know what the Lord wants me to do with the house Aunt Kate left me in her will." She paused for a couple of seconds before going on. "He wants me to turn it into a safehouse for battered women." She announced.

"Are you sure?" Shirley questioned knowing the answer before she asked it.

"Yes, perfectly, I just don't know exactly how to go about doing it." LaRae told the group about finding her Great Aunt Kate's journals and a summary of all she had read in them. After hearing all that her aunt had been through, there was a drawn out silence in the room.

"I know Your Aunt Kate went through a great deal of pain and abuse at the hands of her husband—she was a brave woman to do the things she did—especially in the time period she lived in." The admiration could be heard in Shirley's voice as she spoke.

"Yes, she was," Mr. Potts, agreed.

A quite lull fell over the room once more and LaRae began to think on different situations concerning the house and how it could be made safer for the women that would one day be living in it. She was mainly thinking, never noticing she had started thinking out loud where the others could hear her.

"I know where the house is situated is a perfect place, because there is only one way in and out. I'll need to put up security fencing around three sides because there's a steep hill on the fourth side. I'll need to install a security gate across the driveway closer to the house. Oh, I'll, probably, need to put up some security lights, too."

"I know the name of a respectable fencing company, if you want me to get in touch with them for you." Jason interrupted her thoughts. "They would also install the security gate for you." Startled for a moment, LaRae gathered her thoughts.

"Yes, please do and let me know the date of the appointment you are able to set up with them."

Excited that LaRae would be caring on the legacy her great aunt had birthed out of tragedy and wanting to help as much as he could, Mr. Potts mentioned, "I have a friend who can do the security lighting for you and any handyman work you might need him to do."

"I don't want the ladies to feel like they are in a prison but yet; I want them to feel safe—I believe adding these minor security measures will do that for them."

"What are you going to call the place?" Shirley enquired

LaRae thought for only a moment, "Sanctuary, that's what first the attic was for Aunt Kate, then the whole house after Uncle Joe died; then that's what it became for me. That's where my healing took place." She became quite for a few minutes then declared. "It will be a sanctuary a safe place for hurting women to come and be healed of their past hurts; a place where they can find hope healing and a new life just as I have done."

"A place like that's needed around here, women have nowhere to go to in this area; so they end up going back to their abusive husbands and boyfriends. And the charges against those men always end up being dropped." Jason declared.

"There's only one small problem," she confessed.

"What's that?" the group asked simultaneously.

Downhearted and seeing her dreams dissipating in the wind yet; in her heart of heart she knew this was what God had told her to do, she professed, "I don't know anything about running a counseling center of this type."

Professor Cove spoke up immediately. "I have this counselor friend at the college, who also has a degree in business, which told me the other day, over lunch, she felt the Lord was dealing with her to move into another position away from the college." He looked at LaRae then told her. "I can talk to my friend tomorrow, if you want me too."

Her heart leaped for joy inside of her chest on hearing Professor Cove's words. "That would be wonderful!" LaRae looked at the group then spoke, "Everyone pray that if this is the woman the Lord wants as the director over the Sanctuary then she will accept the position." They all agreed to pray that night.

When LaRae opened the door promptly at nine o'clock, a tall medium weight, light colored skinned, black woman greeted her with a smile. Less than halfway into the interview, LaRae knew two things about the pleasant woman sitting before her, one she joyfully loved the Lord and second she had the skills needed for the position of director over Sanctuary. When LaRae gave Ms. Odom a tour about the soon to be safe house she noted how the women bubbled over with enthusiasm over her love for the Lord and how she found beauty in all of God's creation. She loved talking about the Lord and all He had done for her. If LaRae ever had any doubts concerning this woman and her holding the position of director over this safe haven for women, they were all erased after spending a few hours with her.

At the end of two weeks, contracts had been signed and work had begun on making Sanctuary a truly safe haven for women; LaRae also had met with and hired Ruthie Odom, the now new director over Sanctuary.

LaRae was determined to give women an alternative to staying in an abusive relationship. Jason and her own attorney, David Skinner, walked her and Ruthie, the new director, through the legal steps to be taken by each of the women, which came through the safe house. David volunteered to represent each of the women in court for a small fee, which would be paid out of the house's funds. The Sanctuary would provide counselors, spiritual healing, help with obtaining restraining orders, an attorney, and even if it becomes necessary get them out of state through the Underground Railroad, just as her Great Aunt Kate had done in her time. LaRae made a promise to herself that with God's help she would keep the women safe and make sure they would never have to keep looking over their shoulder, as she had, for so many years.

David Skinner notified LaRae a second check had been received from James' attorneys in Boston of which she endorsed it and deposited the check into the Sanctuary account to pay for the work being done at the house. Part of the front room had been included with the entryway and closed in to make a reception area with heavy doors installed to block the rest of the house off. Some of the larger bedroom had been divided to make two rooms. When the construction was completed the house ended up with eight bedrooms two larger ones for women that might have children. The living room, dining room and kitchen were left intact; all the rest of the downstairs rooms were turned into offices for staff and two rooms were fixed up for overnight staff members.

With construction drawing to a completion LaRae and Ruthie decided to go on a shopping spree; because LaRae wanted to be sure every room gave off an air of cheerfulness. They shopped for each room as if they were decorating their own home, meticulously picking bedspreads, sheets, curtains, rugs, and pictures. Every item placed in each room had to be unique—it had to convey to the woman that occupied that room—see you're someone special—so you deserve to be treated special.

By late evening LaRae was maneuvering her car up the long twisting driveway to the house. Parking as close as she could to the front door, the two women emerged from the car and walked to the back to unload all the sacks and boxes, which held their recent purchases, to carry into the house. After making three trips from the car and up the stairs to complete the task, the women headed to the kitchen for something cool to drink. LaRae was surprised to see a familiar face sitting on a bar stool as they entered the kitchen.

"Well...hello," LaRae stuttered at the site of Cindy.

"Hi." Cindy tried to act nonchalant, but unable to contain herself jumped off the stool and ran to hug her friend. "Nice job you're doing around here."

After introducing Ruthie Odom to Cindy, LaRae had to ask. "What are you doing here, not that you're not welcome?"

"After getting your letter, which explained your strange behavior and all that you had been through, I decided to come and help. I leased out the ranch, packed my things, and her I am."

"Just like that...you're here."

"Of course, where else would I be?" Cindy looked at her friend. "Have you forgotten that I have a PhD in psychiatry? I can be of some help here."

"There's another one of our prayers answered." Ruthie was bubbling over with joy. "Look what my Jesus has done." Ruthie looked at the two women standing in the room with her. "If anyone has any doubt that it's God will for this safehouse to be built, they had better go somewhere else and talk doubt; because God is behind this all the way. He has preformed miracle after miracle around here." The two women agreed with her and they all gave thanks and praise to the Lord for all He had done.

The Sanctuary was officially opened, though officials only knew this. The small staff of counselors was highly trained in dealing with the type of emotional and mental problems the women would be going through. The rooms were ready to receive the women. The basement had been set up as a stockroom, which held clothing and other necessary items for those women whom escaped with only the clothing on their back. There was a well-stocked kitchen of nourishing food for group meal times.

Four days after the safe house had opened Jason brought in the first resident straight from the hospital. Her name was Torah Ann. She had lived through a brutal beating given to her by her husband, which left her with a slight concussion and her left arm in a cast; due to being broken in two places.

While Jason took the paper work into the office for Ruthie, LaRae and Cindy lead Torah upstairs to a room.

"What's your favorite color?" Cindy asked as the three women topped the stairs.

"Yellow…I think" The young woman stuttered, afraid of giving the wrong answer and then being punished for it. Cindy and LaRae lead Torah down the hall to the door outside of the second room on the left. Cindy reached out and opened the door then stepped back and allowed the young woman to cross the threshold into the room by herself. "It's beautiful!" she exclaimed trying to take in the beauty of it all.

Cindy left the two women alone and allowed LaRae to explain some of the rules to Torah. "This is your own personal room, your space, while you're here; no one has the right to enter it without your permission. I know you're tired so I'll let you rest until supper time, but there is one rule you need to know for now the others will be explained to you tomorrow. You can't make any outgoing phone calls at this time. This rule is for your own safety as well as the safety of all in this house. Is this agreeable to you?"

"Yes, that's fine; I don't have anyone to call anyway."

"I'll come get you in time to eat. Is that okay with you?"

"Yes, thank you." As LaRae left the room closing the door softly behind her, she said a quick prayer for the Lord to be with Torah and to show Himself to be real to her throughout her stay here in Sanctuary.

Within three months the house was full and some of the women that had been in the home the longest were showing significant progress spiritually, emotionally, and mentally. These ladies helped in group meetings with some of the other women; who found it hard to open up about their past experiences. The Sanctuary has had three women that had to be slipped through the Underground Railroad to distant unknown relatives because of continues brutal attacks and stalking. The police department in each town got word back to Jason that *the package was received and delivered.*

LaRae's work for Sanctuary took her outside of the home. Most of the women never finished high school or if they had a high school diploma, that's where their education stopped, also most of the women were never allowed to work outside of the home. She took it upon herself to set up educational opportunities, job training opportunities, whatever it took to help these women become self sufficient. She visited the college, trade schools, and different businesses in the area. With her attorney's help she set up scholarships at the college and trade schools specifically for abused women. She was going to do everything in her power to help these women.

LaRae made arrangements to buy the bakery shop that Mr. Abraham had closed down after the death of his wife, Helen. In doing so she found out from the realtor handling the property that the Abraham house was also up for sale. After thinking about the idea for a few days she agreed to look at the house and property, and she was glad she did.

The drive had taken them a short distance outside of town. As they left the highway and traveled down a country road, the countryside's rolling hills were heavily treed with cedars, maples, and oaks, with a variety of wildflowers growing along the roadside. Eventually the realtor turned her car onto a graveled driveway. Soon the driveway curved to the right bringing into view a two-and-a-half-story frame house. A separate garage stood back some distance behind the house. The house and surrounding buildings were situated in the center of a full acre of a well-manicured emerald green lawn. When LaRae saw the place, all doubt had been erased; she knew this was the place for her.

It only took three weeks for LaRae to be moved out of Sanctuary into her new home, have supplies ordered, delivered, and the bakery shop opened for business. Since Torah Ann's ex-husband was now serving time for bank robbery and no longer posed a threat to her, LaRae hired her to work in the bakery shop; now named *The Little Baker's Shop.* LaRae would get up early so she could do all the baking and Torah Ann would run the counter area of the shop freeing up LaRae to do any advocacy work she needed to do on behave of Sanctuary. Within two weeks of LaRae's opening the bakery shop Torah Ann moved into the house with LaRae opening up another room at the safehouse.

One hot summer day while business was slow a petite young girl walked into the shop wearing a pair of large dark sunglasses, a long sleeve shirt, and long loose, fitting sweat pants. Torah Ann noticed as the young woman entered the shop she never removed the sunglasses from her face. She also found it odd that on such a hot day the woman had the long sleeve shirt buttoned up to the neck. As she slowly approached the counter Torah Ann greeted her with a smile.

"Good morning. How can I help you?" Torah Ann noticed the young woman was nervous and kept looking through the pastries displayed behind the glass cabinet and over her shoulder to the blue car parked in front of the shop.

"I don't see them." The young woman on the verge of panic replied in a soft voice, barely above a whisper.

"What are you looking for? Maybe I can help."

"Chocolate éclairs, he said it had to be chocolate éclairs."

Torah Ann recognizing the fear and the symptoms of domestic abuse tried to calm the woman. "I believe we have some fresh ones just out of the oven still in the kitchen. Let me go check for you. I'll be right back." Torah Ann hurried into the kitchen to talk to LaRae.

"There's a young woman out front that I think you need to see." Torah Ann paused and looked at LaRae with tears in her eyes. "She's one of us." LaRae knew immediately what she meant by those words. "She needs some chocolate éclairs and she's being watched from a car parked in front of the shop."

LaRae picked up the tray of fresh éclairs and before heading out to the front of the shop she turned to Torah Ann. "Wipe your face and follow me I'll need you to run interference incase he enters the shop." LaRae put on a big smile and entered the swinging doors.

"Sorry to keep you waiting. Is this what you're looking for?" LaRae asked as she placed the tray of fresh éclairs on the shelf behind the glass.

"Oh, yes, thank you. I need four please." Relief could be heard in her voice when she spoke.

LaRae turned to speak to Torah Ann. "Please fix her order while I take the money." The woman followed LaRae to the register area while Torah Ann boxed up the order. She held out the money in her hand to pay for the order but instead LaRae told her, "Fold that up real small and put it down in your bra, understand?"

"Oh, no, I'm not allowed…" her words trailed off.

"To have money of your own," LaRae finished the unspoken words as she did she slipped her own money out of the pocket of the apron she was wearing and placed it in the register handing the woman back the exact change. "He will be expecting his change back." She looked at the woman then softly asked her, "What is your name?"

"Terri, Terri Carter." The young customer answered lowering the sunglasses just enough for LaRae to see the bruises on the left side of her face then quickly putting then back in place.

"What's you're husband's name?"

175

Terri looked down at the floor and faintly answered. "He's not my husband. He's my boyfriend, Gary Turner." She then defended. "But we're supposed to get married when he saves up enough money."

She then picked up one of the shops business cards turned it over and wrote her personal phone number on it. "I have to talk fast. Don't panic or he will know something is up, understand?" The young woman shook her head in acknowledgement. "I wrote my phone number on back of this card if you ever need help call me any time. He is coming in—follow my lead—don't panic." LaRae took the order from Torah Ann just as the man entered the shop. "Again please accept my apologies for detaining you. I have placed my initials on the front of this card and have written on the back twenty-percent off for your next purchase. Oh, I also put my phone number on the card incase you want to call in a special order." LaRae looked at the young woman praying the Lord strengthen her. LaRae paper clipped the card to the outside edge of the box and handed it to the customer. "Again thank you for your patience."

LaRae watched as the young customer slowly walked toward the man and he grabbed her by the upper arm and escorted her out of the shop. Once the couple was outside of the shop LaRae continued to watch them through the shop window. The man took the box of fresh baked goodies from the young woman and shoved her into the car and slammed the car door; he then walked around to the driver's side and entered the car. LaRae then noticed once he was in the car, the first thing he did was take the business card from the box and turn it over and read the back of it. He did this twice before handing it to the woman.

Sheriff Blanks entered the shop just around closing time at his usual time to pick up his Aunt Shirley's order, which she had called in earlier in the day.

"Evening Ladies," he greeted upon entering the shop.

"Evening Sheriff," Torah Ann greeted.

"Evening Jason, here's Shirley's order." LaRae handed him three white boxes stacked and neatly tied together with twine. "Got a minute?" Jason noting the concern look on her face knew it was important.

"For you, always." He walked over to one of the tables and waited for her to take a seat before sitting down beside her. "What's up? The look on your face tells me it's serious."

"Do you know a Gary Turner?"

"Yes, and he's bad news. We've had a few run-ins with him."

"Any of them to do with Terri?" Jason just looked at her and before he could answer her she launched into her story. "She was in her today and her face was swollen from a beating from someone, most likely him I would guess after seeing the way he treated her. I gave her one of my business cards with my personal phone number on the back of it incase she ever needed help." She saw the worried look immediately when it crossed Jason's face. "Don't worry I covered for her and me."

"I'll see what I can find out. We've arrested him before but his family bails him out before we can get Terri somewhere safe." He eases out of the chair and begins to pace the floor. "His family won't let Terri out of their sight and we've been told she has no family in the area."

Two weeks later Jason Blanks enters the bakery shop around noon. Concern was written all over his face. LaRae crossed the room and met him half way. "What's wrong?"

"Terri Carter has just been brought in to the emergency room." Not knowing how to tell her but straight out he continued. "She's been beat up pretty bad."

LaRae gasped and grabbed her mouth; tears gathered in her eyes as she began to weep for the young woman. "And Gary...?" She asked

"He's been arrested—but he won't be there for long—his parents are on their way to the jail to bail him out."

"If they're at the jail I'm headed to the hospital." LaRae

announced. "Torah Ann you…" She didn't get to finish the sentence.

"Don't worry about the shop. Go, and check on Terri. Everything will be fine here." Torah Ann butted in.

LaRae turned to Jason as they were exiting the shop. "Delay as long as you can so I can have some time with Terri without him or his family present."

"I'll do everything I can—and I'll be praying for Terri too."

"Thank you."

LaRae arrived at the hospital just as the nurse was helping Terri into bed. The doctor had decided to keep her over night. LaRae noticed a cast on the woman's right arm and many bruises covered her face and left arm. LaRae walked up to the nurse and handed her a business card. It was one of her Domestic Abuse Counselor cards. The nurse welcomed her in. LaRae asked the nurse not to allow any visitors to enter the room until she had completed her visit with Terri. LaRae spoke softly as she approached the bed. "Terri do you remember me?" Terri turned her head and looked at LaRae then slightly shook her head in acknowledgement. LaRae had a long visit with Terri finding out information such as; her father had died five years ago and mother's name and where she lived; she also promised to visit the next day. On the way out LaRae stopped by the nurse's desk and talked with the charge nurse informing her of the situation concerning Terri and asked if a no visitor's sign could be put up. LaRae stressed the point of the importance of keeping Gary Turner and his family away from her. The charge nurse said she would talk to the patient's doctor; in the meantime she would put up a family-only sign on the door.

When it turned out Terri's stay in the hospital was extended LaRae visited with Terri daily and as far as she knew Gary or his family had not returned to the hospital, after that first day when they were told the patient could not have visitors except for family. LaRae talk frequently to Terri about domestic abuse to help her understand that it was not her fault. The day before she was discharged from the hospital LaRae talked to Terri about entering a safehouse and the services available for her in one. Terri agreed. LaRae left feeling good knowing this young woman would at last be safe.

The next morning around ten o'clock LaRae arrived at the hospital to pick Terri up. Walking down the hall to Terri's room she noticed Gary standing outside her room in the hallway. Never acknowledging Gary, LaRae immediately quickened her steps and entered the room closing the door behind her. The nurse helping the young woman into her cloths looked up as LaRae entered the room.

"What's going on Terri? Why is Gary here?" She almost hissed at the woman.

"He came to pick me up and take me home?" The young woman would never look up from the floor. LaRae could see that she was consumed with fear.

"How did he know you were being discharged today?"

"He called last night." She slapped at the tears, which were rolling down her cheeks. "He promised things would be different this time. He promised he would never hit me again." Just as she completed the sentence the door opened and in walked Gary.

"Are you just about ready Sweetheart?"

Terri put on a forced smile, "Just about."

The nurse turned to face Gary, "We just about have her ready, but you'll have to wait outside until we've completed the discharge." After watching him leave the room, the nurse had Terri finish signing the papers she held in her hands.

"Terri, are you sure you want to go home with him? Because if you don't I can still get you out of here and into a safehouse."

"He did promise that this time things would be different—I have to give him that chance—he deserves another chance—he loves me."

"What about you—what do you deserve?"

"He promised…"

"Just promise me you will call if you need help—I don't care what time of the day or night it is."

"I promise. But I think this time things are going to be different." With those words the nurse helped Terri into the wheelchair and rolled her out of the room down the hall where Gary fell in step beside them.

A week to the day of Terri's discharge from the hospital Sheriff Blanks and two other deputies were answering a domestic disturbance call at Gary Turner's residence. Pulling his patrol car into the driveway, Jason noticed Gary outside of the house beside his car wiping his hands on a rag. He exited his car and slowly approached Gary.

"Hi Gary." Jason immediately noticed Gary had blood splattered over the front of his shirt. "What's going on Gary?"

"Nothing Sheriff." Looking down and seeing the blood on the front of his shirt Gary added, "Just been doing some bird hunting."

The neighbor that called in the report said a woman could be heard screaming in excruciating pain. Jason was worried for Terri's safety. "Where's Terri?"

"She's in the house. She doesn't want to be disturbed"

Jason started walking toward the house. "I need to talk to her."

Gary became angry and yelled at Sheriff Blanks. "No, I told you, you can't she's asleep and doesn't want to be disturbed." Gary instantly tried to block Jason from entering the house. The two other deputies grabbed Gary, wrestled him to the ground where they applied handcuffs. He was then stood to his feet and searched; in doing so the deputies found a pair of bloody brass knuckles in his front pocket. After searching him, Gary was then placed in one of the patrol cars

Jason cautiously entered the Turner home calling out for Terri. She was found lying on the bedroom floor half clothed and unconscious. She had been brutally beaten beyond recognition. Jason placed a call in for the paramedics and by the time they arrived she had stopped breathing twice. Terri never regained consciousness; she died in the emergency room. Terri was dead, now came the hard part; Jason had to tell LaRae.

LaRae was sitting on the back porch two days after hearing of

Terri's death; she was still mourning the loss when Torah Ann informed her she had guest, three women, one of which was Terri's mother. She wiped her face, entered the kitchen through the screen door, and proceeded through the house to the front room to greet the women.

"Hello I'm LaRae Jones."

The three women stood and the one in the center reached out her hand in friendship and spoke, "I'm Loretta Carter I spoke to you on the phone when you called. Sheriff Blanks told us how to get to your house. These are my friends Debora and Norma." She pointed to each lady as she spoke her name.

"Please have a seat." LaRae gestured toward the sofa where the ladies were seated. "Would you like a glass of ice tea?" Not waiting for an answer LaRae turned to Torah Ann and asked her to please bring four glasses of tea. "Now how can I help you?" LaRae asked as she served each lady a glass of tea from the tray Torah Ann had brought and placed on the coffee table.

Loretta Carter's words came out brokenly; LaRae could feel the anguish as she spoke. "I've been trying to find my daughter for three years. When I finally found out where Gary's family lived and called they told me she wasn't there. She…she was there all the time." She couldn't hold back the tears any longer. "I knew he was bad for her straight away, but she just wouldn't listen to me." She had stood up and was pacing the floor by this time, turning to look at LaRae she continues, "My posed and graceful daughter all of a sudden after meeting Gary becomes clumsy; according to him she was always running into things or tripping and falling. Just about Every night she came home with bruises on her and when I questioned her about them I always got the same answer, 'I tripped and fell', and I tried to keep her away from him because he was so much older than her. She was only sixteen and he was twenty back then. But that didn't work, I came home from work and she was gone." Loretta could no longer hold back all her emotions and broke down in front of LaRae falling to her knees.

"It's okay, mourn for your child." LaRae wrapped her arms around the woman and rocked her gently back and forth until all her tears were spent. She helped Loretta up off the floor and back to the sofa to have a seat between her friends.

Loretta with a serious look upon her face turned to LaRae and asked, "Will you speak at Terri's memorial?"

LaRae surprised by the request spoke gently to Loretta, "But I didn't know Terri well enough to speak personally about her."

"I know you didn't—but you do know about what killed her—domestic abuse."

The friend introduced as Norma spoke up, "We live in the state of Washington and volunteer for an organization against domestic abuse; that's why it took Loretta so long to get here when you called last week. Her own car broke down and was in the shop being fixed so we had to have Debora bring us, who in turn had to request time off from work."

Debora butted into the conversation, "We all know about domestic abuse. Sheriff Blanks told us about all you're doing around here to help the women in this area, that's why Loretta wants you to speak at Terri's memorial. Will you do it?"

LaRae thought only for a moment, "Yes, I'll speak out for Terri and others like her."

The day of Terri's memorial services the urn holding her ashes was placed on a table in front of the funeral home chapel with a large picture of her displayed on an easel beside the table. An organist played some of Terri's favorite hymns, as the town's people quietly entered the chapel. Pastor Jenkins performed the service followed by Kathy, Terri's best friend left behind in Washington, read a poem she had written to Terri; she was followed by several speaking of Terri's wonderful character. Pastor Jenkins stepped back up behind the podium and announced that LaRae would be speaking next at the request of Terri's mother.

After stepping to the podium, LaRae looked down at the urn holding Terri's ashes then to the picture displayed on the easel before looking back up and beginning to speak.

"Terri never made it to true womanhood for she was only nineteen years old when she died. She will never know what it means to be a mother or a grandmother because her life was devalued so greatly by her abuser that it meant nothing to him to take it. Her life was snuffed out instantly with no thought of remorse because her life wasn't her own; it had been taken from her. She had become property not a humanbeing.

Domestic violence and emotional abuse are behaviors used by one person in a relationship to control another. Do you know that every nine seconds a woman is assulted and battered in this country, and 5.3 million women are abused each year, and that Domestic Violence is the single major cause of injury to women, more than muggings and car accidents combined. Fifty percent of all women murdered in the United States are killed by a spouse or an intamate partner. Also, over 500,000 women are stalked by an intimate partner each year. An average of about four women per day dies because of domestic violence. So you see on the day Terri died at the hands of her abuser so did three other women. Three other families in this country lost a mother, a sister, a daughter, an aunt, or a niece.

Terri Carter is not the first nor will she be the last this town will gather together in mouring over. I wish she would be the last, I pray she would be, but until this community starts changing and becoming aware of domestic violence; there will be more victims likeTerri. Think about it! The next service could even be held for one of your family members…maybe even one of your daughters." LaRae slowly scanned the faces of the people gathered in the chapel, in hopes that her well made points hit home with them, before she walked away from the podium and back to her seat to wait for Pastor Jenkins' closing of the service. After tearfully bidding Lorettea and her friends goodbye, LaRae walked across the street to the small church and entered the chapel, unaware of the fact that Shirley and Jason had followed her.

She walked up to the alter and knelt down pouring out her heart, mourning over the lose of Terri at such a young age and many other women whose lives were cut short because of domestic violance. She wept and wept for all the women even though she didn't know them personally by name, she knew all too well about domestic violance.

When she could weep no more for the souls of the women taken by abuse she started to thank the Lord for His protection of her through her own abusive times.

"I know now Lord it was you all the time—you hid me and protected me. You guarded my life to fulfill a special purpose you have for me. I also know that I had to experience some of the thing I went through to be able to fulfill the purpose you have chosen for my life." She also thanked Him for the people He had brought into her life, which helped lead her to Him. They will also help her fulfill the purpose the Lord had called her to do. She rose from the alter knowing beyond a shadow of a doubt what her purose in life is; It is to help women of domestic violence find hope, healing and a new life in the Lord. Because she couldn't save anyone nor could she heal them; she could only point them to the one who could. Only He can heal a broken heart; only He can save a lost soul and give new life. LaRae turned to walk out of the chapel only to see her dear friends waiting and watching over her as always.

THIS HEART OF MINE

Gathering every tiny part, I carefully pack away my broken heart
I build a wall, making sure it is strong and tall
I enter in, my life's in a downward spin
I lock the door, no hurt—no pain—no more
I break the key; this is where I want to be
I am safe, this is my hiding place
I tremble in fear, my eyes overflow with tears
Will my life forever be stained by all this hurt and pain?
Suddenly you appear and wipe away all my tears
With outstretched arms, you offer love not harm
In fear I push you away, I cannot stay
No, not this time, it is too soon for this heat of mine
I must not let you in; it is too painful to trust again
I dare not, open my heart
It will take time to mend this heart of mine
I pray that one-day
On eagle's wings I'll soar, and my heart will know love once more
Some day, but not today